TANUJA RAMACHANDRAN: HUNTER-SEEKER

The Hunter-Seeker Series:

TANUJA RAMACHANDRAN: HUNTER-SEEKER

#26 THE STANK OF EVIL

Kumar Sivasubramanian

Cover art by Mute (mute-art.com)
Developmental Editing by Lu Sexton (lusexton.com)
Proofreading by Sophie Wallace
          (www.facebook.com/SophieWallaceProofreading)
Print and eBook formatting and layout by Polgarus Studio
          (www.polgarusstudio.com)

First edition
ISBN 978-0-9925831-1-8 (Paperback)
ISBN 978-0-9925831-3-2 (eBook)

Dedicated to Mom, Sivagami, Madhavi, and Geeta

1

Imagine a hat made out of cheese. A man makes these cheese hats. What good are they? Who wants them? No one. A way to deal with all your cheese, I guess. But the cheese hat maker, hell, he's forgot how to do anything but make cheese hats. No good for anything else. So one day you're going to end up with a room full of them, stinking the place up, suffocating you, and you're going to have to face the music. What we've got on our hands here is a cheese hat maker. Only she doesn't make cheese hats. She fills chumps full of lead.
Srikanth Jayalakshmi, transcribed from a secret recording made on the occasion of his dismissal in the office of his successor Leopold Vishwanathan

October, 2013.

Though it was doomed to all go wrong, she couldn't have asked for a better killing ground. In Montreal's old, abandoned, and dilapidated warehouse district a woman could slaughter people by the dozens with as much gunfire and screaming as she wanted, and no one would give a shit. After the GFC the entire area had gone to seed and had since been replaced by a more modern industrial park closer to the highways that connected Montreal to New Brunswick, the rest of Quebec, and Ontario. Some of the old factories and warehouses were full of Montreal's most fecund wildlife – cockroaches, rats, pigeons, raccoons, squatters. Some sank under the icy weight of the black autumn sky and could be heard groaning for death even from a distance.

This one looked just as dilapidated but was guarded by a gate and, at the building's entrance, two young men of south Indian descent on watch. They were dressed like bouncers at a Mumbai doof doof club that could be heard for blocks around. Their guns should have been hidden, but they both held them out for anyone to see, fingers on the triggers like they were the latches on the red barrier rope. The power to decide whether you were good looking enough to go inside and get drunk to "Word Up" by Cameo was entirely in their hands.

And yet despite this Tanuja Ramachandran walked right towards them, the cool breeze caressing and shifting her dark sari as she moved. At first, they didn't even see her, even though it was their only job, because they were too busy philosophizing.

"Rajiv!" the younger man said. "Do you think Princess Kate's baby is cute?"

The reply came from the angular silhouette of Rajiv in the dim moonlight. "Shut up, you piece of shit."

"It's so cold, Rajiv. I need to talk for distraction."

"Who the fuck is Princess Kate?"

"She's Princess Diana's daughter! She married the baldy. Don't you know anything?! She had a baby, baby George, just a few months ago!"

Tanuja's spectral figure melted out of the darkness and the two men became all business, guns pointed at her, in the same instant. Both of them had killed before, back in Chennai, in the slums and in the alleys.

"Stop right there!" the royalist commanded. "You shouldn't be in here, lady!"

"Who the shit are you?" spat Rajiv.

As she came closer, the first man's brow crinkled. "Rajiv," he whispered, "didn't Mr. Banerji say something about a woman in a sari?"

Rajiv remembered something like that, but what was it? It didn't seem important at the time. Mr. Banerji was a great man, an important man, but he could sometimes go off on long tangents.

"I thought Vijay was guarding the gate," the younger one said, whispering again.

Rajiv had thought of that too. It could be nothing. What could this woman do to that truck-sized man Vijay? Nothing. Maybe he went for a piss. Right…?

"Stop or we'll shoot!"

It was too late. In the next second she clamped one hand over the younger one's mouth, then decapitated Rajiv with an ornate eight-inch, three-hundred-year-old blade that came out of her purse. The weapon went back into her purse in the same second. The young man stood frozen in place, his eyes as round as *laddoos*, as if he were held there by a beam of fire shooting out of the poppy red *pottu* on her forehead. When he finally found the presence of mind to pull the trigger, she took the gun out of his hands before he could, like it had only been held there with Velcro.

"She's no princess," she told him. Then she flicked her wrist, and the crunch of his neck filled the air like a mushroom cloud.

The sound of his body slumping to the ground was followed by the clopping of hooves. Tanuja looked up and saw Lakshmibai, the *Rani* (queen) of Jhansi, up on her horse Sarangi, in full *sowar* cavalry armor, and with her nine-year-old son tied to her back so he didn't fall off. Lakshmibai wobbled her head at Tanuja and smiled approvingly. "Very best!" she proclaimed, but her breath made no vapor in the cold autumn air because she wasn't there. "Now go inside," the Rani ordered, "and kill the rest of them."

***

Inside, Tanuja shot the first thug right in the pee-pee.

With only the distant light spilling from the office at the other end of the factory floor to work with, she was off target. Rather than being dead, the sentry crumpled into a Freudian fetal position, his hopes for future generations leaking out onto the factory floor.

The gunshot and his screams attracted a dozen alarmed troopers spilling in from other parts of the factory. They were former militia men who'd come from across the subcontinent, now rudderless *gunda* thugs. Many were raw recruits, but motivated enough to drag their asses all the way to Montreal. The jokers were armed with buck hunting rifles. They were runtish too. *Pickings must be getting slim*, Tanuja thought between blasts. Some of the older ones recognized her and threw down their guns and fled. The others kept swarming down between the aisles created by rows of partial mannequins suspended from overhead runners like a robotic meat locker.

There was no adrenalin rush for her as they toppled in dead clumps. It was like riding the same roller coaster over and over again. There was just the sense of compulsion.

Tanuja switched her Vittsjo 727 to semi auto and swooped forward spraying the room, her ropy, panther-like biceps throbbing as the machinegun roiled and the rounds churned through flesh. Through her earplugs the sound was like a continuous subterranean thudding that could be ignored, but she scrunched her nose at the stench of processed plastic permeating the gunpowder. With each dive, swivel, and weave, her braid swung to and fro, and the loose end over the shoulder – the *pallu* – of her onyx black and azure sari flapped violently. Her index finger pulsed against the trigger.

Around her, the haughty, headless mannequins and disembodied plastic limbs watched with indifference, the unlucky ones exploding into powder when the bullets smashed into them.

Her clip would be empty in a matter of seconds. Enough rounds had hit the mark that she was at least slowing them down. But something was creeping in at the edge of her awareness. These thugs, these *gundas*, were staying up for longer than they normally did – some were even getting back up again – and it was draining more of her stamina than she'd expected. For an instant, the thought of her meds flashed into her consciousness. She hadn't taken her prescription for her sleeping problem because it worsened her aim, but now regret was creeping in. There were three men still standing, plus one she'd lost track of. *Sloppy*. One of them she shot clear through the head, and could swear she saw a tuft of fur fly out. That was unusual.

To her left she spotted a door with a small window at eye level. She went in and locked the door behind her to regroup and reload. Inside there was enough light coming in from street lamps outside to make out well-cluttered work benches, sanders, rows of work aprons and filter masks, plaster and paint stains everywhere, scattered plastic arms and legs and heads and torsos. She heard the voices of the *gundas* outside shouting at each other, coordinating the hunt. Then she noticed a door on another wall of the room.

Before she could process it, she dove behind a workbench and the door burst open. Men poured in firing in chaotic bursts, turning everything they hit into dust. They all stopped to reload at the same time, and it was the last thing they ever did.

Tanuja went back out through the door they'd opened for her, and which led back out onto the factory floor and the aisles of plastic bodies. She tossed the now empty Vittsjo aside, and in the same instant the thug she'd lost track of from before pounced on her from the side, four limbs together with the acrobatic precision of a spider.

Her head cracked against a conveyer belt, then the concrete floor. She found herself staring up at the marble-smooth crotch of a bald mannequin with blue eye shadow, but everything screamed yellow and crimson. When the spider leaped on her again, her conditioned body blindly caught him midair in a *kalaripayattu* grapple and swung him to the ground, while using him as a counterweight to flip herself upright. In the next instant, the *pallu* of her sari was around his neck, and a second later came the snap and the slump of death.

She scrambled for cover behind some of the long shut-down factory equipment, and pulled a Bastig .45 from the small of her back that had been tucked into her underskirt. Two men were still firing at her. When she wiped her forehead, the back of her hand came away slick with blood. Without looking, she pointed the Bastig backwards over her shoulder and emptied the clip.

She dared a peek around the machine and could see panic in the lit office at the other end of the factory floor. People gathering documents, smashing computers, and fleeing. But there was order to the panic: directing the chaos was a tall gentleman from Kerala with a vulture-like face and a sharp suit, still composed but rushing them out the door with barked commands. She cursed under her breath and reloaded. When their boss disappeared through the back door of the office, the gunmen on the factory floor started to pull back too, as if pulled in his wake. She took the opportunity to leap out.

The shots from her pistol screamed and flashed in the darkness, like gunpowder-filled hamsters smashed with a hammer. The men fell in the strobe-like flashes of light from their own weapons.

Tanuja charged up the steps to the office, the steel stairs clanging under her sandals, and went through the back door, following the Keralan's path. It opened onto a short corridor with a stairwell visible behind a door still swinging at one end. She went through it and up to the roof.

Up there in the autumn darkness, everything frosted by the gleam of reflected moonlight, the vulture man was climbing into a helicopter. But the chopper wasn't going to start. She'd seen to that well beforehand. Even now, the Keralan was yelling at the pilot as he looked at the controls in dismay. They turned towards her as she came out of the stairwell. The Keralan ducked out of the way and the pilot started to pull a machine gun from under his seat. Tanuja got him on her third shot.

It seemed to be over. The Keralan straightened and watched her walk towards him, as though he were an unmoving planetary body pulling her into his gravitational field. He remained as still as a meditating *sannyasi*. This was how he was going to die? So be it.

"Banerji," she said flatly, as if naming this moment, the moment of his death. But a few meters away from him she stopped. She rubbed her eyes with one hand, the other still pointing the gun at him. Then she looked at his sneering face with a scowl of her own, lowered the gun like a rag doll, and then crumpled to the ground and had a sleep.

***

The plate on the door of the office in the embassy building read "Leopold Vishwanathan." The plate on the oak desk said "Leopold Vishwanathan." But the woman sitting behind that desk and across from Tanuja was not Leopold Vishwanathan. She was Nandhini Shastri: tall, straight-backed, with a noble face. She was a silver-haired elder stateswoman with a storied career at the embassy, and a laugh that charmed weaker minds. She was impossible to like.

They had not said one word to each other since Tanuja had entered the office two minutes earlier and Shastri gestured for her to sit. The stillness was a relief to her aching, bruised muscles. Just that morning, she'd slept with a man whose name she couldn't remember to calm her nerves, but it hadn't helped. And Rani Lakshimibai hadn't approved.

Behind Shastri, leaning against the shelf of antique leather-bound Indian classics, was a mousy, clear-skinned man with a round face and a smug expression. He was a few years younger than Tanuja, and he wore a cheap suit. His presence drew a sneer from Tanuja of a slightly different angle than the "I smell a fart" sneer she usually had on her face.

Shastri sat with her index fingers steepled over her lips, staring at Tanuja. On the desk was a manila folder with her name stenciled on it. Outside the arched windows, the skies over Montreal were a milky Cadbury purple™, leaden and inedible.

Tanuja didn't need to be told what had happened to Leopold, but when Shastri broke the silence in her clear, authoritative voice, she told her anyway.

"Leopold Vishwanathan has been let go."

"So Leo got fired, and you got demoted?" Tanuja asked.

If Shastri was stung by the insult, she buried any sign of it so deep she'd be shitting it out within the hour, and went on unperturbed. "You were his project, and frankly I'd rather not have to resort to employing a forty-year-old narcoleptic mercenary."

"It's not technically narcolepsy —"

"I know that, Miss Ramachandran, from our previous torturous conversations. And we've all read your dossier." She flipped it open and rifled through it. Even in 2013, Indian bureaucracy dragged everything down onto paper. "Six months undercover in Kabul at age sixteen, four years in Kashmir. One year fighting in a Gorkha military unit. Oxford educated. Black ops in Sri Lanka. Somehow had time for a family in between all that. Assignments all over for the Indian government before settling in Montreal in 2004. Black-belt-level martial artist in *kalaripayattu*, *silambam*, and *varma adi*. Firearms expertise level eight." She held up a medical page and squinted at. "Some *thing* that's basically narcolepsy. Narcopha-something. None of which exonerates you from the boner you pulled in this operation." There was a snicker from behind her.

"*Dey*! The intelligence was garbage," Tanuja said. "There was nothing right about it except the spelling. There were more men there than I was told to expect. And they seemed… strange." The words were a lure, but Shastri did not take the bait.

"If Leopold screwed you, why do you care so much that he's gone?"

"Who said I cared? He was the lesser of two evils. Besides, his information came from *higher up*."

Shastri gave her an avuncular smile. In all their

encounters, this was the closest Tanuja had ever seen her come to flinching. "Nevertheless," she continued, "*you* fell asleep and Banerji got away. Perhaps the most notorious terrorist in India's history. You fell *asleep. You fell asleep.*" She tapped out the words in an angry, corrupted Morse code on her desk as she spoke. "You cocked this up." Another guffaw from the little man behind her.

"I finish my missions. I'll finish this one."

"Despite the bad intel?" she taunted. Shastri nodded to herself for a long moment, her mind working. Finally she said out loud, "I would hire someone else but you've killed most of them."

Tanuja cackled, genuinely. Apart from the dossier on the desk between them, everything that happened in this office was off the books. Some of the top embassy officials had gotten into the habit of employing mercenaries to solve certain problems. It worked, even if higher ups like Shastri didn't always like to admit it. But it was all so illegal that the hired guns effectively had the advantage. If their embassy handlers didn't meet their demands, they could threaten to go public. The embassy could barely complain about anything. Unless a personality like Shastri's was in play. "Guess who hired me to kill those people?" Tanuja asked.

"We're in the business of troubleshooting before trouble shoots us," Shastri conceded. It was also effectively the reason the embassy was trying to crush

Banerji themselves instead of reporting his presence in the country to the Canadian Secret Intelligence Service – if it got out that a nefarious Indian terrorist was on Canadian soil, every Indian and Brown person nationwide would suffer for it.

Tanuja had the upper hand now. "I'll do it –"

"Of course you will," Shastri interrupted.

"But I want the truth this time."

"You already know it." Shastri said nothing more, but did not break eye contact with her.

There was a kind of hazy stirring in Tanuja's solar plexus. She spoke for Shastri. "2001…?"

"Yes," she admitted.

"I killed *that thing*." All three in the room knew what "that thing" was: a strange creature known as The Monkey Man of New Delhi.

"Yes," Shastri said. "But the man we think created it was a man named Dr. Srikanth Balu. Bioengineer. We thought he had been liquidated, but…" Shastri gestured and the mousy man behind her passed her another folder. "He's alive. And he's here now in Canada. Whatever weirdness is going on with Banerji's men, Balu is likely the one responsible."

Shastri took out a photo and slid it to Tanuja. It was a surveillance picture of a Caucasian man from the waist up, standing in front of the front steps of what looked like a large, Victorian house. There were a few young, brown-skinned security men in the shot too. The photo looked to have been taken with a telephoto lens through the bars of a gated driveway. The man was somewhat tall and scruffy, with a horseish face and wearing a t-shirt. He looked like a hacker or a soda jerk or both.

The man behind Shastri finally spoke. He had an unusual, subdued accent. Tanuja found his presence in the room as annoying as Shastri's and let her crinkled brow tell him so. "The cake is Pete Smith," he said. "We've received intel and intercepted some communications that point strongly to Dr. Balu visiting Smith's estate in Fredericton, New Brunswick multiple times over the past year or so."

"Do you have a picture of this Balu?"

The man behind Shastri shook his head. "Not even from his university records back in India. He's covered his tracks."

"What's Smith's deal?" Tanuja asked.

"He's independently wealthy. Inherited. And he runs a roller derby outfit."

Tanuja knitted her brow.

"I know," Shastri answered. "It doesn't make any sense to us either. That's all we got from our connections at CSIS and our own surveillance. Actually, he's a public figure, bit of a local hero. We could have just as easily put a newspaper clipping in that file. But it seems to us that Balu has been doing… something to Banerji's men. Balu created that thing in 2001, and you fought Banerji's men last night. They were no ordinary men. Now we have reports of Balu visiting Smith. So figure out the Balu-Smith connection and you'll find Banerji. You finally get Balu. I finally get Banerji. The world gets rid of them both."

"I want this mission. And I want twenty-five thousand dollars," Tanuja announced.

Shastri's eyebrows arched in disbelief. She looked at the man behind her. He was laughing outright.

"You can have ten thousand," Shastri said smiling, "plus expenses. No wonder Leopold almost exhausted his budget. You could have been living like a raj in Tamil Nadu all these years with that kind of money!"

Tanuja's face was an anvil.

Shastri conceded. "Okay, fifteen thousand. We wouldn't want you to starve. And we don't meet here anymore. Another of Leopold's incomprehensible oversights."

"One other thing," Shastri said. "This is Akshay 'Max' Lakshmanan." She gestured to the man behind him. "He's coming with you. My eyes and ears to make sure you don't louse this up again. He'll also be your field medic. I'm told he knows what he's doing. He asked for the assignment. Only Vishnu knows why. In any case, maybe you won't get killed."

Max finger-gunned her. "It's short for… Maximum!" he smiled. Shastri gave him an exasperated grimace.

Tanuja snorted. "Didn't it used to be Maximum Pervert?" The opportunity to insult him finally handed to her on a platter, she relished it, staring holes through his skull. *What a little weasel.*

Shastri's eyes darted between them. "You two know each other?"

"He's my brother," Tanuja said.

Shastri scowled, lifted the Tanuja Ramachandran dossier, and dropped it into the bin with an emotionless clank. The sound was a reverberating confession of the never-ending failure of Indo-Canadian intelligence.

Tanuja buttoned the photo into her purse, and got up to leave. Shastri was rubbing her temples in silence with her left hand.

"See you in the morning, sis!"

"One more thing," Shastri said as she was at the door. When she stopped and turned, Shastri said, "Take your goddamn medication this time."

***

When she got home, Tanuja sat in the dark with her eyes closed and listened to two Vilayat Khan sitar albums in a row through state-of-the-art headphones – her one indulgence. The sound system was the best that money could buy, and if not for its monolithic glory anyone walking into her two-bedroom apartment might have assumed she was squatting there: used furniture, just a mattress, no bed, a sometimes cacophonous thirty-year-old fridge she maintained herself, two plates, two forks, two spoons, peeling paint in every room. The bedroom was small. Big enough to sleep in, listen to music, and shimmy around the mattress to the closet. Not much else. You wouldn't get much larger right on Rue Sainte-Catherine.

Outside her window on Rue Sainte-Catherine she could sense the night crowds oozing through the night from one Tim Hortons to the next, sex shop to sex shop, desperation to desperation. Around the stoop of her building West Africans sat laughing in disbelief at the twists of Fortune as all the headlights crawled past them, families in a cycle of consumption, couples, singles, the whole of life in a slow motion dusk-lit swarm.

She had had enough music after the first album, but found herself unable to move for the longest time. It took a monumental effort of will to pull off the headphones and toss them onto the mattress. For a while, she sat and replayed memories of the family she once had, like a toy projector in her mind. Like a curse. All the good things, and that horrible ending. She massaged her forehead as if that made it any better. Whenever she wasn't "working," this is what consumed her thoughts. This is what sent her to work again. The things gone forever.

She unwrapped her sari, the blouse, and petticoat, and went into the bathroom in her underwear. In the mirror she examined herself. The strong aquiline nose. The void black eyes. She angled her left shoulder towards the glass and felt the top of the scar. It was about three inches wide at the top and crossed her left breast, tapering down to a point just above her solar plexus. Under the gentle touch of her calloused finger tips, the disfigured flesh was a rocky Martian landscape, like hardened lava, brown and bacon red and purple.

She closed her eyes, and in the blackness she remembered the creature that gave it to her: humanoid, covered with tufts of coarse brown fur, four-inch steel claws on every finger, and wearing a green metal helmet. An otherworldly screech issued through its fangs, and when Tanuja opened her eyes, it was standing in front of her in the mirror, its hot panting breath in her face, the smell of it. She didn't take her eyes from the creature, and as she glared, the miasmic stirring within her solar plexus that she had felt since she sat in Leopold's office accelerated, swirled, and coalesced into a tiny marble-hard sphere, equal parts fear and vengefulness. Her voice was an iron rasp.

"Monkey... Man..."

2

Upon entry to the scene, arriving investigators and EMTs found the body of Ravneet Mahesh, male age 29. The body was located in the living room and killed with a machete. The Mahesh-Ramachandran children, ages 6 and 4, were found dead in the corridor. Tanuja Ramachandran, the mother of the children, was found in the rear garden of the property, suffering gunshot and knife wounds and in a state of cardiac arrest. It is believed Mrs. Ramachandran, rumored to be a government operative, may have been the primary target. To date, no arrests have been made in the case. Based on certain evidence, it has been speculated that one of the perpetrators was Kamal Natarajan, lieutenant in the Paayum Puli terrorist organization. Natarajan was himself found dismembered in May 1998. Ramachandran case file #170165, first opened January 1998

To a giant, the world might look flat, but to She – a tiny ant, perched on her six legs – it was a three-dimensional universe of colossal craggy, broken features. In the littered forest undergrowth ahead of her, every leaf, every rock was an obstacle of mountainous dimensions. An incline an inch high was a summit beyond which nothing could be seen until She scampered clear to the top. But her body was built to walk upside down on glass if she wanted too. Her legs, like hydraulic pistons, sped over the topography with tactical precision.

She was a part of a trail with her sisters, hundreds of them, half still heading out to the find, but half – like She – heading back to the hive with one of their stomachs full and sated for herself, and the other stomach full to provide for the colony. Where She and her sisters passed through the patches of sunlight that peeked through the canopy of foliage so inconceivably high overhead, a pinprick glint reflected through each hairy segment of exoskeleton, creating two squirming lines of armored, microscopic red-brown lights passing each other, antennae forever swiveling and twisting in the air.

She did not "think" about any of this. She was more body than mind, a system of programmed, predetermined chemical and physiological reactions. She was herself, but She was not an individual. She was Us. She was more than just a unit. Tens of thousands all together, each She of the colony was like a cell or neuron of a collective brain.

Until a few days ago, She had been lazing in the hive, doing nothing since She'd hatched but eat every day, fed and pampered. Then her antennae had smelled that it was finally her time. From that moment, she was a forager, and every day since she had gone out with her sisters to do as the scouts signaled them to do. The scouts were her sisters too. They were all sisters. Today, a scout had gone ahead, found something – something significant – and sped back to the colony, retracing her own steps. When the scout returned, she gave some of the foragers a taste with vomitous kisses, and then the foragers had headed out, sniffing out the scout's strengthened double-scented trail with their antennae. As all the foragers followed the trail and came back again, the trail smell became stronger still and even more of her sisters became compelled to follow, an automatic reaction to the scent in their antennae.

At their destination, the foragers had found a bee hive, shattered on the ground, perhaps knocked down by a bear. The dead bees were everywhere. Speed was of the essence. Us was more than ten meters from home. Another colony could find the broken hive at any moment.

Us had charged in at the flailing, wounded bees, rocking back and forth pathetically like Gregor Samsa, and sank their mandibles deep into them. They drank their fill of the bees' juices, filling their two stomachs to capacity, and then turned around and headed home along the smell trail to return the food in their social stomachs to the colony. The colony would probably eat ten million such dead and dying insects this year.

But as She and her sisters got closer to home, it became evident something was wrong. She heard a chirping distress call from the guards at the entryway. When She got there, the entrance to the hive was damaged – crumbled and smashed apart – and some workers were already repairing it, but her home Sisters were all in confusion. And as she got even closer to the entrance and touched antennae with the others there, too many were soldiers. The soldier smell reached a critical mass, tripping a chemical switch in her, and She too suddenly became a soldier.

The sisters She had returned with were becoming soldiers too. They scurried deeper into the tunnel system, but in only a few moments they came upon Mother.

No. Each of Us had two eyes and these eyes had many eyes within them, but even so She still could not see so well, especially here in the dark of the tunnels. It was hard to tell in the dark, but this great creature before them did not look quite like Mother. Although, like Mother, it was big enough to have smashed through the hive entrance creating that chaos Us had passed coming in. The instant after She and her sisters saw this Other Mother they charged to attack, but their antennae smelled it in that instant and, yes, it was

Mother. It had to be. It smelled of Mother. If She was capable of thought, She would have wondered why Mother was way up here by the hive entrance. No matter. It was Mother now. It was Now-Mother. Now-Mother, who had birthed She and all of her sisters and brothers in waiting, who was now their Mother and had always been their Mother. Now-Mother shifted and looked at them but remained where she sat.

The hive entrance was broken, there were soldiers everywhere, this did not look like Mother, and it should not have been in this place, but to Us's robotic unit-brains none of this data was possible or even acknowledgeable information. Only the scent was information. And then there was another smell, a smell that triggered a chemical recoil through their bodies that sent Us into confusion again, turning, bumping into each other, until the chemical frenzy inside each of them congealed into a kind of unthinking, mechanical incandescent fury. The stink of it! Coming from deep down in the tunnels!

It had all passed in a few seconds. Us had hardly looked at Now-Mother and already Us had swiveled and turned, continuing on deeper into the tunnels at a frenetic pace towards the horrible stench – the stench of an intruder. An intruder there to kill Now-Mother!

Deep in the bowels of the hive, Us found her. Another creature might have recognized this as Then-Mother, this massive thing, belly so swollen with eggs she was hardly able to move. She turned slowly in the deep dark and sniffed the air with the equivalent of resignation as her daughters charged at her, hearing them through the vibrations in the ground. This close to the intruder stench, She and her sisters had no control over their brutal rage. She was pure physiology, no more than a system of organic reactions. This thing was in their hive to kill their Mother! Us smelled it and felt the chemical equivalent of an emotion: a defensive fury. They "hated" it! Glistening mouths tensed open with bear-trap-like tension, She and her sisters fell upon Then-Mother in a ferocious wrathful swarm. Ultimately, the act would mean the end of She and her sisters all within two to five years. With barbed mandibles sharp enough to cut through a beetle's black armor, She started sawing off her own mother's head while her sisters carved her to pieces in total abandon.

3

I can state – and will *state here for the record – unequivocally that the Indian Embassy in Montreal does not and has never engaged in the types of criminal activities described by this Commission, I find the very notion of this "vigilantism" as the Honourable Minister Bouchard chooses to call it distasteful in the extreme.*
Nandhini Shastri, statement before the Royal Commission on Uncanadian Activities, 2012

Grundtal .221 Repeater, black and beetle-like. Minimum recoil but inaccurate at long range. Still, she'd used it once to shoot both a man's arms off before kicking him onto a helicopter rotor. By that definition, she found it effective.

1971 Datid M60. Total overkill, but if you're a cannibal, the world's most efficient way to make hamburger. She took it down off the rack.

Skogaby SARL – surface-to-air rocket launcher. It

had a sleek, futuristic look. Could prove useful, but wouldn't fit in her luggage. She left it.

Roknas Lite. A 9mm handgun that was a good fit for her purse or under her pillow. Twice she'd used it to liquidate targets in already compromising situations. She decided to take it.

Graddig 42. Robotic in appearance, unthinking. It was a machinegun of Finnish origin whose design hadn't changed since WWII, and in her experience was less likely to jam than its Russian equivalent, the Kalashnikov. It came off the rack with a clatter.

She took the weapons out of the hidden panel in her closet into the kitchen, lining them up on the table in a perfect row. When she finished, she noticed the Rani sitting in the chair with its peeling vinyl seat beside the table and her son on her lap. Lakshmibai always waited until Tanuja was alone before she showed herself. The boy immediately scuttled off to play elsewhere when Tanuja looked at them. She set her sword on the table beside Tanuja's weapons and glanced over them. She wobbled her head in conditional approval.

"Not bad," she said. "But you know I don't care much for this modern… *machinery*. When I fought Captain Heneage I had no such things. Only my sword. It's going to be really special this time, don't you think? Important, not like your usual jobs. Killing the scumbags that kill innocent people, like the ones that killed your family – that is the mission. But that

Monkey Man, that scary thing that hurt you so badly… We never really knew the truth about him. But now finally you can have your *revenge*."

"You're saying I should kill them with ceremony?" Tanuja asked.

Lakshmibai snapped her fingers with a smile, jingling her bangles. "You took the words right out of my mouth, Tanuja! Very best. Why kill them quickly? Let them feel it for a while."

Tanuja nodded. "Yes, I'll do that." She turned to go back to the closet to get some of her more exotic weapons, but Lakshmibai interrupted her.

"But why are you still working for those embassy people, Tanuja?"

"What difference does it make? Who do you think pays for all this?" Tanuja said, eyeing the guns.

"I don't like that Shastri."

"Old boss, new boss," Tanuja said, but there was no force in her words. Lakshimbai replied with her eyebrows.

"Did you know your brother was working for Shastri?" Lakshmibai asked, her words needle sharp.

"No. When was the last time I talked to him? I didn't know if he was even still working with the embassy." Tanuja was on the defensive. She knew it. The Rani was cornering her.

"It feels like a betrayal, doesn't it?"

Tanuja only looked at her.

"Maybe his betrayal is even worse than you know.

Why do you keep protecting him? Perhaps you should kill him too." Lakshmibai's expression was unreadable but her eyes twinkled, reflecting lights that weren't in this room or any other.

"Max is all I've got, however little that is," Tanuja said, looking at the array of hardware on the table. When she looked up again, the Rani was gone. Tanuja exhaled. Sometimes the Rani said unthinkable things in the most casual or gleeful way. It took Tanuja a second to get over her surprise. Then she went back to the closet for more weapons.

***

The day after they'd been in Shastri's office, Max came over to Tanuja's and they loaded up her '68 Charger for the drive to Fredericton. The duffel bag full of hardware was so heavy it visibly weighed down the trunk. This didn't surprise Max, but it did seem more than usual. She allowed him to put one bag in the trunk as well, but before he got into the passenger seat she pointed at the carrier bag over his shoulder and said, "You haven't got that fucking Casio in there, have you?" It was an ominous question in the grimy, echoing parking garage where she could liquidate him and no one would ever find out about it. Still, while he knew she was paranoid, could she ever really go that far?

"No," he lied.

"It's a six-hour drive to Fredericton," she said. He

took it to mean: I understand that's a long time to be without your keyboard.

But what she meant was: I can't endure your Casio playing for six hours. "You're lying," she said.

He actually squared his feet and put his shoulders back. "As you know," he said, "I need my music to sublimate my guilt. It's the only thing that works." He didn't even know what "sublimate" meant, but there had been an incident at work, and his therapist in the subsequent mandatory counselling and sensitivity workshops had used the word.

Tanuja slapped him – *dishum!* – and put him in a headlock. "Screw off! Screw off!" he cried. Tears started to well up in his eyes, but he wouldn't concede. Finally, she twisted him around so she could grope around in the bag herself and retrieve the offending instrument. It was a slightly larger one – nineteen white keys and thirteen black. She smashed it against a concrete post, and after the tinkling stopped, said, "Get in."

He smoothed out his hair and clothes and did as he was told, but once they got out onto the highway and she really had to focus on the road, he pulled out a smaller seventeen and twelve key Casio from the same bag with a look of haughty indifference, as if she weren't even in the car with him. When she saw it, her nostrils flared and her *pottu* seemed to too. Her fingers gripped the wheel like tarantula legs.

"How many of those things do you have?" she grunted.

"How many people have you killed?" He actually gave her a second to think about it, as if it were not a rhetorical question, before he cut back in. "Answer: lots. The place to get them is garage sales or – even better – deceased estate sales."

"I don't kill people at garage sales," she said.

"But you would. And maybe I've even bought some at estate sales that I have you to thank for." He started playing some discordant notes. Any second now the singing would start. "See? It's all connected. And that's exactly why I stayed up half the night writing a song for just this occasion. To make it up to you."

"How long have you been working for Shastri?" she asked, eyes on the road.

"See, I knew you were going to ask me that. I knew you'd be angry. A couple of months. You and I haven't worked together in a while." He played three chords that had no business appearing in succession. "I heard the buzz around the office that Leopold was going to get the axe. I ingratiated myself with Shastri to protect myself. I guess I really am a grown-up now," he said with a twinge of nostalgia in his voice. "In the old days, it would have been you that came to my rescue and got me another post so Leopold didn't take me down with him. Not anymore. Anyway, it's that simple."

"To protect yourself?" she asked. "No. I think you just wanted to get to see the mission files even earlier than you did with Leopold. Well? Did you like what you saw?" she sneered. It was a challenge, not a question.

She didn't like to talk about whatever it was that happened in New Delhi in 2001. Almost as little as she liked talking about the catastrophe that happened with her family. "There wasn't much in it," he said. "Obviously."

"Obviously."

But it was enough. He was lucky he saw the file when he did, however thin it was, because…

"You're here to monitor me and report back to Shastri."

Max could sense the red heat of her paranoia. He wondered what would happen if she ever perceived him as a threat or a perpetrator of wrongdoing, one of the endless parade of scum bags she gleefully erased from the universe. But he refused to let it phase him. "I'm on *your* side! Does it really matter that I didn't tell you right away?"

"Two months is plenty of time, Max."

"*You* could have called *me* too."

"*Dey*! This isn't a game, Max! There will be knives, guns, bombs." She stopped short of saying "mutants" out loud even if Shastri herself had suggested the possibility.

"And that's another reason why you need me. To patch you up."

"Just like the old days."

"Just like the old days. And you need *me* too, Nooj. Every time I see you, you're worse than ever. You're… you're losing it."

"Shut up," she said.

They didn't say anything for a minute. He noodled the Casio keys. Finally, he said, "Are you ready to hear my song?"

"Never."

"The only thing is," he barreled on, "I couldn't fit in any of the stuff about how those spooky guys took you away from the orphanage when you were ten, and then a few weeks after that I got adopted by the family in Canada, yada, yada, yada. And then how you showed up five years later hanging around outside the fence of my school like a creepazoid, and you were only fifteen but you looked like the entire cast of *Predator* combined. I mean, what rhymes with 'predator'?"

"Sexual predator."

"I don't think you understand how rhyming works." F major 7th.

"I don't think you understand how songs work."

"I don't think you understand how life works!" he cried.

That day at his school in Brampton, she confirmed what he'd always suspected: that it was her that had gotten him out of the orphanage somehow. After they reconnected, he saw her every few years, but she never seemed her age or like she'd experienced any youth at all.

His song didn't have any lyrics about her family either. But he often wondered about the nature of it. Maybe she had gotten married so young in a desperate attempt to obtain that missing normalcy. At least it distracted her from the mess he was making of his own life at the time. Either way, it all ended in the most horrific way imaginable. After that, whatever was left after the death of their parents, whatever her own little family had planted back into her, that was all gone too. She was a wraith. And then the 2001 business happened in Delhi. One of the things had made her psychotic, the other had made her paranoid, but he couldn't say which went with which.

In any case, she would be aflame with a fury for vengeance. If she went on this mission alone and unchecked, whatever sanity she had left would be gone forever, and there would be no coming back this time. Right now, there was still hope for her. She found beauty in things, like that horribly twangy sitar music, and… various types of guns. That was something wasn't it? A sign of the spark of life?

The Casio music started, and for a flash of an instant Tanuja was surprised, then realized it was just the one of the preset demo tunes, a jaunty, tinny 80s beat that would have been right at home on a Mini Pops album. She made a swipe for keyboard, swerving the car along with her, but he twisted his body towards the window and she only caught air.

Here it comes, she thought. "For fuck's sake." In fact, his songwriting had very little to do with sublimating his guilt, a fact she knew since he had been wailing nonsense and marching around banging on pots and pans consistently since he was four. The amazing thing was the lack of improvement.

"This song is called 'Remember,'" he said. "Oooh!" he began, but then he had to sing very fast to keep up with the Mini Pops tempo.

My name is Akshay and I'm here to say
My sister kills chumps in a different way!
There was a time when you used to be nice!
Even in the place with the mice and the lice!
Then you were gone! That's the end of the song!
What the heck's wrong? Don't you like them that long?
It's not over yet! A gun in your purse!
And Brampton's center of the universe!
And you checked in on me from time to time!
Don't eat that burger! It's beef and cheese slime!
Thought I'd be a veterinarian!
Was that a bad choice for an Indian?
So you got me in, but I got kicked out!
Now let me tell you what that was about!
I got kicked out 'cause I did the bad thing!
Which do you prefer, MySpace or my Bing!
But you saved me again with a sweet deal!
Both of us vets, got the embassy feels!

It went on and on like this, longer than all of Tolkien's elf and dwarf songs combined. The drive to Fredericton should have been eight hours in a "normal" car, or six hours in the Charger. She did it in five and a half.

***

Within a half hour of leaving Montreal they were already in farm country, driving from smell to smell: cow pastures, horses, skunks. As they got closer to Fredericton, they drove through a town that smelled entirely of French fries. She tried to imagine the isolated, mote-like lives being lived in these places. But then she visualized the world from space and *all* humans and *all* cities became invisible. She saw the Milky Way and the Earth became nothing. She saw some form of the universe and even the galaxy vanished. Human action became nonexistent and inconsequential as though it had failed to exist on the most quantum level to begin with. Not even sound, not even fury. She kept her eyes on the road and drove into forever. She could hear the clip clop of the Rani's horse following them at some distance behind, urging her not to slow down.

Late that night, they drove through a tiny town cradled by rolling hills just outside Fredericton. The main drag was a strip of pretty shops and restaurants: charming in summer, apocalyptic in winter. Further out was a loose network of weatherboard houses, many from the 1930s or earlier which the townsfolk had maintained as well as could be expected in a communal attempt to try to keep the place quaint. Church steeples stabbed the sky.

Tanuja pulled up at a gas station where the highway left the town for the last leg to Fredericton.

She had started to fill the tank when Max popped

out the passenger side. "That was excruciating!" he accused, and her eyes went wide. "I've been trying to break through to you for two hours, and you're still giving me the cold shoulder! You're unbelievable! No – I take that back. I believe it. I should have known. That's on me. But I told you I'm sorry. I wrote you a song. I told you about those girls that dumped me, and how I drink too much, and my 'friends' from work, and all that stuff. That's me baring my soul. And what do I get?" he said, slamming the door shut.

"It's been five hours," she said.

"Five…?"

She hung up the gas nozzle, turned, and walked, sari swishing, into the sagging, peeling station. Max followed like a puppy.

The glass door tinkled when they went through it. The stocky middle-aged woman behind the counter folded up her newspaper and stood up to serve her. There was no one else in the shop. Max went over to the magazine rack and looked at the covers.

"You must be a new one!" the woman said to Tanuja, her eyes wide and smiling.

"Pump number one," Tanuja said, her words slowed by her surprise and confusion.

"Sure thing! That'll be $78.50!"

She handed her a hundred. Max had wandered over to a community bulletin board. While the woman rung up Tanuja's money, she chuckled to herself.

"Well, if there's one thing you can say for Pete," the

woman said handing Tanuja her change, "he's *consistent* all right." She chuckled again. "I'll see you tomorrow night then."

"Sure thing," Tanuja parroted.

Back in the car, Tanuja leaned back in the driver's seat and looked up into nothing.

"That was odd," she said. "That woman didn't look twice at my sari. And the things she said…" She trailed off in thought.

"Well, while you were playing social butterfly, I got us our first lead," Max said holding up a flyer he'd picked up inside.

Tanuja took it from him and read it.

Max grinned and said, "Looks like we're going… *to the roller derby!*"

4

The heroes, counting up their days, set down as vain
Each day when they no glorious wound sustain.
Valluvar, Tirukkural couplet #776, circa 450-550 CE

The bout was the next day. They drove around until she found the cruddiest part of town, and then she found the worst motel. It was across the street from a disused service garage surrounded by a dilapidated fence and a gate hanging off the hinges. They parked nearby and she walked over to the ramshackle lot. It was overgrown with weeds and rusting car bodies. She fired a bullet into the air and waited. There were murmurs somewhere, the clatter of dishes, televisions. After half an hour she fired another shot. This time a patrol car showed up twenty-three minutes later, crept through the area, then sped off again. It was perfect. They checked into the motel.

***

The next day, they had some time to kill before the bout. Tanuja wanted to clean her guns, or sit in the car at the venue parking lot. Max spent some time writing songs, then said they should go to the art gallery since they'd come all this way and he'd heard it was a good one with a twelve foot tall Dali painting in it. She agreed, if only to shut him up, and after the guns were clean. Dali's Santiago El Grande was indeed impressive. Saint James on a white steed and the souls of the earthly dead rose up through the clouds on Judgment Day.

"See? Isn't this great?" he asked her as they sat in front of it.

"It certainly is," she said with no emotion. "Who knew you were such an art expert, Max."

Oh, shit, he thought, *here it comes*. He shouldn't have said anything.

"Tell me, Max, what was the last movie you saw? I want to take you up on another of your recommendations."

"Well," he murmured, "it had Katherine Heigl in it…"

Humiliation: Successful.

And yet, Tanuja found herself still thinking about the painting later. For a while, they sat in a park and Tanuja looked through her kaleidoscope, something she often did when deep in thought or trying to distract herself. Wherever they went, she sometimes heard the Rani's horse Sarangi's light snorting or the Rani's bangles or the laugh of her nine-year-old boy.

When Tanuja and Max got to the venue at twilight, the parking lot was nearly packed and the rink was lit up inside and out. The town's cars at least were in better shape than the town's houses. Lots of shiny SUVs, even some meticulously restored vintage cars, and everything in between. There was no way to read the demographic from the vehicles. But Tanuja also guessed there were more people here than from the town itself. There were lots of US plates. They'd have driven a fair way.

Before she got out of the Charger, Tanuja undid her braid and let her hair cascade over her shoulders. Max looked at her quizzically, but she said nothing. It was almost start time, and they were about to follow the straggling spectators inside from the lot when they were accosted by a short pasty-skinned, Caucasian woman. She looked about fifty, was plus-sized, and had stringy hair hastily put in a ponytail. She had been speaking to a group of people on the other side of the lot, but had spotted Max and Tanuja as if by radar. The mere sight of her coming in a missile-like line towards them had frozen Tanuja and Max in their tracks.

"You!" she shouted when she was still only half way across.

She would have gotten right up in Tanuja's face, but Tanuja radiated a force field-like hostility that repelled the woman back a few feet, so she was pacing back and forth in front of her like a caged meerkat, the veins in her head an apoplectic purple, even in the dimming light.

"You're one of Smith's new ones, huh!" she spat. "That fucking cheating cheater! Always trying to cheat! He knows there's no adding new skaters to the roster on bout night! We'll see about this! This shit will be fucking mediated!"

"I don't know what you're talking about," Tanuja said, wide eyed.

"Liar!" she cried, and stormed off.

"Well, that was weird," Max said with a chuckle that betrayed discomfort. Tanuja gave him a look that said, "*Everything* here is weird," and then they both went up to the doors. There was a young Middle Eastern manning the ticket booth. He looked bored to death. When he saw Tanuja, he said, "Why aren't you in uniform? They're almost ready to start," he began, but then stopped himself. "Oh, sorry, I thought you were someone else."

Could this be one of Smith's hired thugs? Tanuja wondered. Somehow connected to Banerji and Balu? But then – why was he selling roller derby tickets? If he was hired muscle, no wonder he was bored.

He appraised her silk sari with a glance. "I suppose you'll want seats in the VIP booth?" he asked.

"There's a VIP booth?"

"Forty dollars," he said.

The venue itself was a massive hockey arena called Willie O'Ree Place. The venue had two rinks, one of which had been converted for roller derby. It was also tricked out with state-of-the-art lighting, disco balls, sound systems, and other fittings. There were eight tiers of stadium seating teeming with toddlers, teens, middle-class families, and some who probably had truck engines and 30-year old sofas and mattresses out on their front lawns, plus students of all colors who'd come up from the university in Fredericton. Oddest of all was the VIP booth, which was occupied by seemingly wealthy spectators who either hadn't bothered to dress down for the event, or were up-jumped rednecks. Tanuja and Max took seats next to two well-dressed women in their fifties drinking wine from Champagne flutes. They looked about as happy to be there as the goons working the door.

They were still getting settled when the crowd erupted.

A burlesque swing descended from the ceiling amidst a wheeling light show, and Pete Smith was on it. As he stepped off it and into the center of the track, the applause died down. He did a ridiculous crotch shaking, arm pinwheeling dance to the applause and laughter of the audience. He looked much as he did in the photo. He was wearing jeans and a t-shirt of Death's 1990 album "Spiritual Healing," with the greed-faced faith healer and the man in the wheelchair. Tanuja thought a small town crowd would be sensitive about something like that, but judging from the reactions around her, it was just another familiar part of Smith's clown act. His hair was untidy, like he'd gotten out of bed and fixed it by running his hand through it once. To Tanuja, he had a face that betrayed perpetual naiveté. His file said he was thirty, but he seemed closer to eighteen.

"To create roller derby," he said, pointing emphatically at different sections of the audience with each word, "one must first create the universe."

"Oh, here we go again," murmured the woman sitting next to Tanuja. Her partner laughed.

"They're inseparable," Smith went on, "like cheese and bacon. And when the skaters go around the track, their qi energy gets blasted back out into the galaxy like jet streams!" During one of his finger points, Smith randomly locked onto Tanuja in the VIP booth and for a moment their eyes met and froze, but he didn't miss a beat. Looking away from her, he continued, "And we are here tonight, as always, to celebrate that cosmic union! To celebrate it with an interleague bout the likes of which has never been seen before!"

The audience cheered.

"Now, as you well know," he stated, "we have had a long-standing rivalry with tonight's visiting team." There were some friendly boos from the crowd. "And some might say – again, and again, and again – that it's unfair somehow that the coach of the home team also owns the home team and the arena in which they're competing, and is also one of the match commentators. My parents left me a legacy. They saw, like I did, that roller derby stood for something. Stood for everything. And it was their wish that I keep the heritage of roller derby alive in this town. Who owns what? These are petty, earthly concerns. Ladies and gentlemen – the fate of the universe is at stake! We are all here to do our best! Our visitors have brought some savage new players with them, but rest assured we're stronger than ever…" Here there was an awkward pause for a flash of a moment, like he'd forgotten the script, or something else. "We're stronger than ever too," he finished. The crowd cheered over his hesitation.

"I know a lot of you guys have come in from all over the place," Pete said, instantly becoming the orator, ringmaster, and pot-inspired metaphysics guru again. At some moments it seemed to Tanuja that he really could be connected to Banerji through Balu. But at others it was inconceivable.

"Thank you especially to our friends from the States." There was cheering and some playful jeers from the crowd. "So I won't keep you long. I want to remind you all that half of everything you spend here tonight – your tickets, t-shirts, food, drinks, everything – goes to the soup kitchens all over New Brunswick." Loud clapping. "That's why the beer's so expensive!" Uproarious laughter. "Jimmy, let's kill these lights!" Pete said gesturing.

The main lights died, and spotlights flooded the track. The roar was deafening. Colored stage lights started to swirl and careen around the venue again.

"Without further ado, please welcome all the way from Bangor, Maine – the Annihiskaterrrsss!" The skaters came out in green and white team colors and swooped around the track like apparitions under the strange colors of the lights. They pulled up at the starting line in tight formation with falcon-like precision.

"And now!" Pete's echoing voice called out. "Your hometown heroes – the Ass! Kickin'! Qarnage Queeeeennnss!!"

Vermillion and black, helmets and pads glistening like armor, the team swung onto the track at breakneck speed. They were not as bulky as the women from Bangor. The Queens were sculptured and more uniform. Several of the Annihiskaters were positively Rubenesque, and many of them were heavily tattooed and had futuristic hairstyles: angular blue sculptures with lightning bolt zigzags dyed into them, or eight-inch mohawks. The Queens were much more conservative, and they were older than the other women too, their faces grim, unfeeling death masks.

And they were all almost all brown.

Tanuja felt a slap of familiarity followed by a constriction in her chest. She had seen them before, but where? Had she seen them in person, actually met them, or seen their photos somewhere? Under the pandemonium of lights it was hard to be sure… They didn't look Indian though.

The sight of them staggered Max too. "What… the… fuck?" he wondered aloud as they swished around the last corner in precision formation to the starting line.

Once she got over the déjà vu, Tanuja's lip curled, and she snorted. She had been harboring a certain hunch since the gas station and it seemed to be turning out to be right.

The starting whistle blew. The orderly formation immediately clumped a ten-player hockey fight. There were two players at the back with a big star on their helmets who shoved and jostled their way through the riot then sped around the track to come up behind the brawl again. Again, they pushed their way through, and now the electronic scoreboard started getting busy while the refs gave hand signals like they were dancing the YMCA. There were a few stops and starts as the whistles blew, but these were mere lulls in the Viking furor. The players with the stars seemed to be winning points by passing the other team's players, but the stars were printed on a kind of bathing cap and sometimes these got passed to another player who would rocket off at twice the speed as the previous owner, leaving the pit fight behind. Sometimes players would fall over and a sickening crack of their helmets would resound through the venue. The one aspect of the rules that Tanuja managed to work out for sure was that the game was played in two "periods," a detail which coaxed a snicker out of her. For an hour the track turned into a nexus of velocity, force, evasion, and navigation at breakneck speeds. The Queens had the upper hand in every respect.

The massacre was punctuated by Pete Smith's relentless frenzied commentary booming out of the PA. "Good god! That was an awesome assist by Axle Rosanna letting Princess Bruise Lines get past and score two more points for the Queens! And – holy shit! That was a heavy duty J-block from Bomb Delouise square into Patty Snake Patty Snake's chest! Meanwhile Sophie's Choice just got a major for tripping Tran Boleyn! That's a minute in the box for Sophie and some seriously unenviable fishnet burn for Anne!"

The woman sitting next to Tanuja caught sight of the confused expression on her face. "You're from out of town?" she asked.

Tanuja nodded.

"This is our fourth time to one of these things," the woman said with a moneyed drawl, "and it still doesn't make any sense to us either. As far as I can tell they just go around in circles and beat the tar out of each other. But, as I'm sure you know," she said, eyeing the threads of Tanuja's sari, "you do better business with Smith if you show an 'interest' in his life's calling. I'm assuming that's why you're here?"

"It's like I keep telling June," the other woman said, indicating the first, "the roller derby's like a firewall blocking any access to Smith's parents' money. They did a poor job with their wills, let me tell you. This town could be thriving if that money had been put into a better arrangement of trusts requiring actual business managers that know a good investment when they see one, rather than this yahoo. Every time we have to go through this," she said, shaking her head.

The first woman continued. "Listen, I don't know your line of work, Miss…"

"Tanuja."

The woman pressed her lips together in a kind of disbelief. "You'll forgive me, but I'm not even going to try to pronounce that. But there's a diner on the south side, right along the river, called The Paradise. Smith owns it and he goes there after every match. If you really want to get into mommy and daddy's money your best bet might be to try to corner him there. You won't have much competition. Most of us dread the thought of the place."

"Thank you," Tanuja said.

"And the Annihiskaters have just ganged up to execute a wicked waterfall on Violentina!" Smith screamed through the speakers.

The skaters flew around the track for the rest of the hour like protons in a particle collider. At the end of it, the Qarnage Queens had lived up to their name and won a bloody victory, while the other team limped bruised and aching off the track.

5

I hate Indians. They are a beastly people with a beastly religion.
Winston Churchill, savior of the Western world, 1943.

After the game, they went to The Paradise diner on the main street on the other side of the river, and found it next door to a weird old cinema. The Paradise was supposed to have good poutine according to Max's phone. Some other spectators from the game went there too. The diner itself was overly lit and crammed with twenty and thirty-year-old video game cabinets at the back. Tanuja made a beeline into the arcade game cacophony towards Street Fighter II while Max put in an order at the counter.

There was a kid playing the machine solo. Tanuja clinked a coin in and took the right side controls. "What's your name?" Tanuja asked her.

"Emma," she answered, her voice edged with nervous trepidation. "Emma Reed."

"How old are you, Emma?"

"I'm eleven."

"I will destroy you, Emma Reed, age eleven."

Tanuja selected Dhalsim, the fire-breathing pacifist yogi. Dhalsim immediately went on a pitiless rampage against Emma's Zangief, the Russian wrestler.

Max showed up with his poutine as Tanuja fed more change into the cabinet. "So what's our play?" he asked with a mouthful of gravy and fries.

"There is no 'our,'" Tanuja said. Emma had chosen the Chinese martial artist Chun-Li. Dhalsim breathed fire at her.

"Okay, what's your play?"

"Smith likes brown women," Tanuja said. Chun Li kneed Dhalsim in the face, ten feet in the air, three times in a row. "I sensed it since the gas station."

Max coughed on a cheese curd. "Yes, anybody can see that, but –" In that instant, the pieces fell into place in Max's mind. His jaw set and the veins stood out in his neck. "Are you…" He could barely bring himself to say it. "Are you going to try to act… all sexy or something?"

Tanuja didn't answer. She just kept pounding the controls.

"Oh, good god! I don't need to hear this! I'm your brother!" In fact, Emma's eyes were just as wide as she listened to them argue.

"*You're* the one that said it!" Tanuja grunted.

"Grody to the Max!" he wailed eponymously.

What next? Would she sit on his head and fart on him? "And another thing – we don't actually know anything about this guy, Nooj! He could be a ninja or some shit for all we know!" He looked at her reproachfully, but being some years her junior, the effect was comical, especially since she wasn't even looking at him. Also, whatever Smith was, if things got hairy, she would just shoot the problem away. As always.

"*Dey!* You're judging me? This from a man who was disgraced for sniffing the sweaty bicycle seats of female colleagues – twice."

Max gasped, appalled that she would say it out loud, explicitly, and in public. His eyes brimmed with tears. "*Zangief! Zangief! Fight like a queen! You have purple pyjamas, if you know what I mean!*" he improvised, but the guilt didn't go away.

Tanuja slapped him – *dishum!* – and the distraction afforded Emma an easy win.

He moved closer to her so the kid wouldn't hear, and gulped down his self-loathing. "Look, it was only *one* colleague, all right?" That was a lie. "There was a rumor she didn't wear any underwear." He regretted saying it as soon as it came out, but he couldn't help it. It was all knotted up with the rest of his pathology.

"Does that mean you sniffed the seat to see *if* it was true, or because you thought it *was* true?" It was the Tanuja Ramachandran equivalent of a joke. A thing approximating a smile appeared on her face, more just a curve of her mouth, like piano wire around your neck. But to Max… it was again the barest evidence of a human being trapped inside her even if only in the form of a dabbler in schadenfreude. Maybe he could pull her back to the normal world after all.

"Nooj, we've got nothing. We saw Pete Smith, from a distance, for a few minutes, first night we came to town. Lucky break —"

"Maybe too lucky," she interrupted.

"What do you mean?"

"We have evidence this fool has been associating with a rogue biologist and possibly also a known terror financier. But he's walking around in broad daylight and hosting roller derbies? Doesn't he have any enemies?"

"So what do you make of it? Is it a trap, or something else? Bravado?"

"It doesn't matter. We follow the clues, Watson, and then we blow out the brains of every scumbag on the planet."

Emma blocked out their conversation as best she could, and fished some more change out of her pocket between games.

"I don't think Sherlock Holmes ever said that. Anyway, we're still empty handed. What about Balu? What about Banerji?"

Tanuja flared. "You want to give *me* lessons on tracking down an enemy? You desk monkey! I know what I'm doing. I couldn't give two shits about Banerji, but I'll have Balu by the throat if it's the last thing I do. Why don't you go back to the motel and phone *that* report to Shastri!" *Perhaps you should kill him*, the Rani had said.

A crowd had started to form around Tanuja and Emma, some to watch the video game, some to hear more about the seat sniffing.

There was some commotion at the restaurant end of The Paradise. Tanuja turned to see Pete Smith coming in with group of Queens, as expected. He waved at the patrons that saw him and the cooks behind the counter. The Queens started occupying any booths they could find. Despite being there to celebrate a victory, they looked about as happy as soldiers sitting down to vacuum-packed rations, but the diner was now even more packed and noisy.

Pete had stopped to talk to some people, but one of the Queens – a big one – was making her way towards the arcade games. For a while, she stood with the crowd with her arms crossed and watched in silence. She had all the charm of Stonehenge in November. Max tried to avoid making eye contact with her, but she stuck out like an ogre surrounded by dwarfs.

The Queen watched Tanuja win two more matches. Emma lost badly a third time. But before she could put in another coin, the Queen swatted her away like a fly, jammed in some money, and clutched the controls. She rolled her shoulders and cracked her neck, then selected Guile, the US army guy with the crew cut. Tanuja stuck with Dhalsim. The two women never looked at each other. Tanuja didn't need to look at her to know that the Queen's objective was humiliation.

The Queen was mashing the controls before the game had finished announcing "ROUND 1." It was good enough for the Queen to catch Tanuja off-guard and take Round 1. Tanuja won Round 2. The sound of a distant earthquake rumbled out of the Queen's throat.

"Round 3!" the game announced over the blare and jangle of the other machines. The crowd was thick around them now. Most of them seemed to be cheering the local, even Emma despite being shoved out of the way by the Queen only moments earlier. Even Max kind of hoped to see his sister taken down a notch. He was so close to her, he could see how sweaty she was, like she hadn't showered after the roller derby.

This was the round in which Tanuja learned the Queen hadn't been button mashing. Tanuja stole a glance and saw that the Queen's fingers were actually so fast it had just seemed like mashing. Dhalsim went into defense mode, while the crowd cheered his suffering. Even Max's eyes were lit up.

As the blows pummeled away at her, Tanuja inhaled and summoned up the teachings of her *kalaripayattu* master Lalitha Venkateswaran, a woman herself not unlike Dhalsim. The focus took her into the screen, so close to Dhalsim that he became a jumble of meaningless brown pixels. And then she occupied his being, and waited. Waited for the instant to strike. Guile jumped up to do the knee bazooka that would end her. Tanuja leapt up, did a Yoga Smash, flame, spear, and throw in succession. The Queen's anger was palpable, but Guile was down. It only took two standard punches to finish him. The Queen shouted, every vein in her body threatening to burst, and smashed the joystick so hard she broke it off, then smashed the screen with it.

As the two women turned away from the machine, the crowd dispersed, frightened and impressed. When they were gone, only Pete Smith was there. The blustery showmanship he had on display during the roller derby match was completely drained out of him. He looked at the Queen and the damage she'd done to the cabinet with a combination of white-faced alarm, embarrassment, and awe.

"I, uh, I have to apologize for her," he said. "You'd think she'd be in a better mood after winning her match." His tone should have been condemnatory, but he sounded more like he was prodding a bear with a long stick to see if it was asleep.

"It's the management you ought to be apologizing to," Max offered.

"I own the place," Pete said. "My name's Pete Smith." He was looking at Tanuja now. "This is Flora, a.k.a. Heavy Flo."

Flora didn't speak. She just stood there, not the least perturbed.

"I saw you at the game tonight," Pete said. "Up in the VIP booth. But you don't seem familiar. Are you from out of town?"

It was a strange thing to say. The city's population was 50,000. It betrayed what he really meant: *I know every brown woman in this town.* "We're passing through," Tanuja said.

"Okay," Pete said. "As long as you're here, whatever you want, it's on me. By way of apology." He dared a glance at Flora and the shattered machine again. "Look. Can we sit down?" he asked. "This is awkward."

Tanuja nodded. Pete led them to a booth where he sat next to Tanuja, and Max sat next to Flora. "Do you drink beer?" Pete asked. He signaled to someone behind the service counter and they started preparing the order for him without him having to say anything.

Tanuja adjusted her sari over her shoulder. It was tide pool blue with a jasmine and purple vine pattern. Though her downturned eyes, she saw Pete watching her do it with his teeth fixed. They made eye contact, and then he returned to himself.

Tanuja's face changed in a way that Max had only ever witnessed once before. The hardness went out of the muscles and a kind of luminousness came out of the classical, angular qualities of her face. She did not smile, but that not-smile was a kind of smile in itself. Even this second time, Max found the effect was uncanny and transfixing. "Tanuja Ramachandran," she said. "This is my brother Maximum Pervert."

"Is that, uh… Hell, I didn't know they had *men's* roller derby anywhere around here!"

Max was incensed, but Tanuja cut him off before he could say anything. "Never mind him," she said to Pete. "He sniffs bicycle seats. Tonight was –" She stopped mid-sentence and her head slumped down.

"I—is she all right?" Pete asked.

Max shook his head in disgust. "She's just asleep." He leaned across the table, snapped his fingers in her face, and squished her jaw around like a Muppet. "Hey, Nooj! Nooj!" he called. He had to slap her twice – *Dishum! Dishum!* – before she woke up, slapping him back – *dishum!*

"Wow," Pete said.

Tanuja was unphased. "– our first time to see roller derby."

"Well, why just watch the match?" Pete asked. "Come see the team practice tomorrow morning. Maybe you could even join in."

"What?!" This was the first time Flora had spoken. Max was taken aback by it. Tanuja still couldn't place her, but her accent was Middle Eastern. "She's not one of us, Smith!" Flora said behind crunching teeth.

"Flora," he said in that exasperated, flat tone that was more pleading than challenging.

"And what if she falls asleep?" Flora sneered. Tanuja was staring at the woman's face, still too distracted by the déjà vu to retort.

Flora took the stare as arrogance. She pounded the

table with a hammer-like fist that could have forged swords. "You think you're better than me?! Just because you're rockin' a b-cup?!"

"She's right, sis," Max said. "You're being kind of rude to her."

How bizarre for Max to say anything at all in the situation, and to take Flora's side, no less, for no logical reason. What had come over him? "It doesn't matter," she said. "I haven't skated in ages. I'll pass. I used to play lacrosse though. Long time ago." Tanuja fished a quarter out of her purse and said, "Max, why don't you go play Galaga for a minute?"

"Flora, look, maybe you should join him," Pete said. Flora flushed, her chest heaving, but she said nothing and slid out of the booth.

Max swiped the quarter and shot off like a bolt after her.

Pete laughed off Flora's outburst. "The skaters all have minds of their own, you know. Sometimes there's no telling what they'll do next."

Tanuja was about to answer, but Max came back and stood beside the booth. "Galaga's fifty cents," he said. She sighed and threw her coin purse across the restaurant. Max went scrambling after it.

The drinks arrived.

Pete caught Tanuja looking at the logo on his t-shirt and said, "Do you like Death?"

"No."

"Okay." He didn't know how else to respond.

"…"

"They were a seminal death metal band, maybe the most important of all of them, but their main guy, Chuck Schuldiner, died when he was, like, thirty-four."

"Don't you think that's ironic?" Tanuja said.

The callousness of her statement went over Pete's head. Tanuja put her arm up over the back of the booth seat so he'd be able to get a whiff of her armpit.

The nostalgic glaze in his eyes was replaced by a smile that would have been a leer if his face hadn't had that perpetually naïve quality about it. At this rate, she thought, she might end up finding Balu and Banerji without wasting any gunpowder at all. "So tell me, Mr. Smith," she said, interrupting his brief reverie, "Why roller derby?"

"Oh, that's easy," he said. "I tell people all the time. It's the goddamn metaphor of life. You're the jammer, out there all by yourself trying to score some points. Everyone else – they're trying to block you. Stop you from getting what you want. You gotta plow through them. And your team, they're like your family. The ones you should be able to count on, but it's all happening so fast you can hardly tell what's going on yourself half the time. Sometimes I feel like if you can win at roller derby, you can win at life. The principles are all the same."

"I'm not sure that that's true," she said. During his speech, his voice had become low and pregnant.

Tanuja only understood what this idiot was talking about half the time, and really the things he said applied to almost any sport. She was more amazed that anyone could talk to a stranger like this, but two aspects of the man were starting to become clear. One was a tyrannical tunnel vision that took hold of the man and throttled him whenever he started talking about roller derby. The other was a kind of hesitating deference whenever he spoke to Flora. He approached her almost like a trainee lion tamer.

"Anyway," he said, "I've gotta go. I've got this kinda timetable thing I've gotta keep." He waved to Flora, then retracted his arm like he'd waved to the wrong person. "Look," he continued, "if you won't come to practice tomorrow, I'm having a party thing the day after. For the harvest festival. You really ought to come. I want you to come. There's going to be a parade the next day too if you can stay that long. We're going to have a float in it." He sounded proud of that bit. "I'm even having a riverboat lunch thing afterwards." Everything was a "thing" to him. "You could even come to that too." He pulled a gold foil-stamped invitation out of his jeans pocket. It was slightly crinkled, and he smoothed it out with somewhat bashful tenderness.

"I need an invitation?" she asked.

He shrugged. "It's supposed to be sort of a formal thing. It's not really my scene, but when you do lots of business, you have to do this sort of social stuff.

Anyway, why rush out of town, right?"

Tanuja's only reply was a computational blink, and, "I'll think about it."

"That's all I ask," Pete said. Pleased, he got up to go find Flora, who was waiting by the glass doors. Max was back again.

"How'd you do?" Pete said before leaving.

"8,500 points."

"Nice one!" Pete saluted goodbye and then walked away whistling with his hands in his pockets. Tanuja eyed him and Flora all the way to their car parked on the other side of the street, a seemingly mint condition lime green 1974 Bricklin SV-1. Really they looked as innocent as Shaggy and Scooby heading back to the Mystery Machine.

"Well?" Max asked.

"We keep our heads down and wait around until some more of these Queens leave. Then we go buy some beer for minors."

6

Tanuja applied her elite military training to the questioning of four teen-aged mini-Pete Smiths hanging around outside the liquor store that was just up the road from the diner. They were smoking and failing at it under the shop's outdoor lights. They found her sari a curiosity, but they didn't argue with the six pack she offered them.

She discovered the skaters all had rooms in Pete's mansion. One of the punks stopped just shy of admitting he'd been there peeping. She caught a look between two of them that all but confirmed her suspicions, and it pleased her. If a fifteen-year-old could spy on the place, for her it would be as easy as scoring an up-skirt of Miley Cyrus.

***

The estate had heavy security considering how exposed Pete had been at the game, and would have been easy to find even without the address printed on the party invitation. Every other mansion in Fredericton was practically open for hobos. But the front of Pete's was gated with an electronic video security system. Some distance beyond the gate she could see the three-story Victorian mansion with high gables and light spilling out of the windows that provided all the illumination she was likely to get. Two well-groomed brown men were loitering innocuously by the steps up to the front door. Through her binoculars Tanuja spotted the trademark bulge of Gulort 203s under their shirts and realized Pete's security was sourced from the Middle East too. There was a tiny grove of trees and bushes opposite the house, on the other side of the drive that curved to the front of the house and away, and more trees by the four-car garage further back from the house, and along the back too. Plenty of cover once she got in. She got out of the car, and closed the door behind her without saying anything to Max. He watched her with a knuckle over his lips, her black sari like the glimpse of an owl sweeping through the shadows.

An eight-foot high brick wall surrounded the rest of the complex. She followed it around to the right until she found a strong oak on her side almost hugging the wall and with cigarette butts on the ground next to it. This would be the one the teenagers used. Some of the lowest hanging branches had been cut back, but one solid one was still within reach. She spidered up the tree, like a shirtless nine-year-old from Varanasi trying to steal fruit. The Rani egged her on telling her to go faster but more quietly, oblivious to the cacophony of her own jewelry.

Within seconds Tanuja was over the wall, and landing on the ground in a near soundless crouch. Some squirrels and bugs fled at her feet. Staying low behind the bushes, she crept forward along them until she could peek through at the guards and the house. From this vantage point, she could see the appeal for the boys. From here, there was a clear view through the windows and the guards just looked like chauffeurs who at worst would shoo you away or threaten to call the cops. Even now, through one window, she could see one of the Queens eating protein supplement powder straight from the tub like it was ice cream. Through a second floor window, she saw one of the Queens hooking on her bra over a bodybuilder's physique, triceps flexing as she reached behind her. Then Smith entered the frame of the window in a house robe. The pair became half obscured by the window frame again. Tanuja couldn't tell if he was kissing her or speaking closely. Then, Smith walked away, grabbing what looked like a small toolbox off the dresser as he left the room. If Smith was sleeping with the women, it would make things more difficult for Tanuja. But she was somewhat puzzled the woman hadn't been Flora.

One of the guards flicked a cigarette butt in her direction. She slowly backed up, creeping closer to the back end of the mansion. She found another oak. Again, it only took a few agile grabs and bounds, leveraging against the brick wall, to reach a high, sturdy branch. Laying across it, leopard-like, she pulled a pair of binoculars from her purse and peered into the third floor windows on this side.

This time she had not been quite as silent. One of the guards strolled over, a fresh cigarette in his hand. He lit it, then pulled a flashlight from his back pocket and swept the bushes with it. The other guard, still leaning against a column by the front steps, said something to him in Arabic and the near one chuckled. He checked his watch, nodded, and said something short and affirmative back, laughing again. He switched off the flashlight and looked up at the windows. He caught sight of some movement in a top floor window, a flash of dark skin. He backed up to try to get a better view. Still not good enough. He walked towards Tanuja's tree, and started to climb.

Here was a boy who'd probably grown up with artificial rock climbing attractions in shopping malls in Qatar, not the banyan trees of Pondicherry like she had. Though it looked like he'd climbed this one before, it was an awkward affair – he triple checked every foothold before he reached for the next purchase. With each noisy placement, Tanuja slithered back along the branch to the trunk, the leopard in rewind, and ascended to the next sure branch.

Tanuja let the guard continue his noisy climb and looked through the third floor window now directly in her line of sight. One of the Queens was in there, fixing her hair. Her door opened and Pete came in smiling. They stepped beyond the frame of the window and she couldn't see them anymore.

From the branch below her there was a disappointed sigh. The guard had missed the best of the show. Tanuja crept backwards again and descended the trunk like a shadow to his level behind him. But she was not quite silent enough. A branch cracked under her foot. When he spun to look it was too late. His head was already in her hands and slammed hard against the branch. It was a muscle memory reaction, and she didn't even register what she had done until she was looking at the back of his unconscious head.

The guard on the ground called out his comrade's name, but then the front door opened and a woman's voice speaking to the guard prevented him investigating further. A cone of light spilled out from the open door. The guard and the woman continued talking. No doubt, he was making excuses for his friend. Tanuja grabbed the peeping tom around the waist and scrambled down the tree like King Kong.

He was heavy. When she reached the ground with him, she was puffing. She was back in her original position between the bushes and the perimeter wall, and looking at the main entryway from the side. She could see the guard, but the woman he was speaking to was blocked by the architecture. For now, the woman was just a voice. Tanuja looked down at her Fay Wray. She pulled his pants and underwear down to his knees, and left him there face down in the dirt. Ideally, they would find him before he woke up and reconstruct the crime in the way Tanuja hoped.

As she got up from her crouch, the woman at the entrance thumped down the steps. No show of being a chauffeur here. It was one of the Queens, a giantess practically twice Tanuja's size, in army boots and military fatigues. Tanuja froze when she saw her. She had remembered who they were.

Gaddafi's Nuns.

She ducked down again, and started to look for a vantage point to scale back over the wall. They were going to need to call Shastri to send more people from Montreal. Surrendar or Ranganajan at least, maybe more…

Tanuja never saw, heard, or predicted the choke

hold coming, but one second she was breathing, and the next she was desperate for oxygen. She had been veering close to sleep and the choke had the unintended effect of jolting her alert. Even through the supple, feminine flesh of the arm, the imminent lethality of the ursine grip was as palpable as the warmth coming off the flesh in the darkness. She was far stronger than Tanuja, maybe stronger than anybody. It was a larynx-crushing death grip, its intent unmistakable. She could hear a kind of leering pant coming from the Queen behind her. She hadn't sounded any alarm or cried for assistance. She was grinning and waiting for Tanuja to die. *Good.* That meant Tanuja had some time, and since the Queen had had to attack her in a low position, she still had some leverage. But then she felt a knife start to push itself into the flesh in her back...

She was able to kick out backwards into the Queen's shin. There was a grunt of pain – what would have been a shout, but was suppressed by professional training – as the Queen keeled over and lost her grip around Tanuja's neck. Tanuja swivel flipped so she was on top, clamped a hand over the Queen's mouth, kneed her in her jungle area, shoved the back of her head into the dirt, anchored a knee onto her chest, yanked up a nearby squirrel with her free hand, and rammed it into her mouth until the life deflated out of her like a blow up doll.

And the poor squirrel... well, at least its death had

been a memorable one: bitten to death by one of Colonel Muammar Gaddafi's virgin guard.

***

Back at the shitty motel, Tanuja was sitting on the edge of her bed in her bra, rubbing her neck and putting iodine on her scrapes. Max had put stitches in her back where she'd been badly gouged by the knife. Now, he was seated in an uncomfortable, stained chair next to a lamp thirty years out of fashion, scratching his head. They had been sitting in a long silence, but Max broke it.

"Tell me again," he said.

"How is it you work for Shastri and don't know any of this?"

"I'm just trying to get this all straight in my head."

She pressed her lips together and looked at him with her Gorkha-hard eyes before she started. "Colonel Gaddafi kept a personal bodyguard. His most elite troops. Hand-picked out of the Revolutionary Guard Corps. Crack fighters. A cadre of at least forty women known as The Revolutionary Nuns."

"Beautiful virgins."

"Beautiful virgins," she nodded. "Or at least that's what he made them out to be. But you need to understand: when the regime fell, some of them died, and some escaped, but for most of these women, while they worked for him, their lives were *horrific*. Unimaginable. Do you understand what I'm saying, Max?"

"Yes," he answered.

Tanuja could see in his eyes that he *didn't* understand in the least, but she went on anyway. "Most of them vanished. Maybe they went to ground and found the peace and anonymity they craved. A chance to heal and atone. Maybe that's a pipe dream. But some were cut from the same cloth as Gaddafi himself. They scattered too, and the intelligence community lost track of them as well."

"Enter Pete Smith."

Tanuja nodded again. "Gaddafi's death would have devastated them. They would have been completely vulnerable, easy pickings for a new Daddy. I suppose Smith's trying to collect the set."

She capped the iodine bottle and went into the bathroom. Max mulled it over. When she came back, she was dressed in a plain white t-shirt and pajama bottoms.

"What for?" he asked. "The brown fetish? He must've had to track these women down from all over the Middle East. Seems like a lot of time and resources for some women with father complexes."

She sat on the edge of the bed again. "I agree. There's something more to it."

"Or something less."

"What do you mean?" she said

"He may be rich, but that kind of operation doesn't seem to be in his wheelhouse. The guy's crazy for roller derby. He owns the team and the venue, and he announces matches. His money's inherited, he never even earned it himself. Are we really supposed to believe he's associating with rogue scientists and known terrorists? He doesn't seem like the type that thinks three moves ahead."

"No," she agreed, "but maybe two." In her mind, she tried to process Banerji and Balu's connection here, but there were not enough pieces yet. "But then how do we explain the women? *Maybe* they came to *him*," she suggested.

"Maybe," Max agreed. "What about the house?"

"Reinforced glass. Nobody in the house heard anything while that idiot snapped every branch on the way up. Also, Smith visits the women on a regular schedule. The guard knew almost exactly when to climb the tree to get a good show."

"Meaning?"

She shook her head. "Maybe they're used to a routine from their Gaddafi days. Or maybe Smith has pathological habits. Either way, we can use it to our advantage to get in the house. The glass and those guards… there may be something more to the place."

"And you said he did two? In a row? How? He's not *that* young."

"Blue pills maybe?" She rubbed her face.

"And what's the play with the dead woman?"

For the briefest instant, she had to recall what he was talking about. "That I don't know yet." She shifted gears. "What did Shastri say?"

Max pursed his lips. "She said we need to… *apply* for backup. In writing." He paused for effect. "By post."

She grunted once in disbelief, then again in frustration. But it was the Indian embassy. It was not surprising in the least. Even the fact that – despite the mission being off the books – they demanded paperwork.

"According to Shastri's intel," Max said, "Balu is connected to Banerji and Smith is somehow connected to Balu. Wouldn't your normal MO at this stage be to point a gun at Smith's head and ask him about Balu?"

"Max, I've dealt with so many scumbags, wiped their ugly faces off the face of the Earth, but Pete Smith… You said it yourself. Something's off. Does he care about anything except roller derby? What if the intel's bad, again? Threatening him might do more harm than good." She *was* beginning to reconsider Smith. Maybe he wasn't as dumb as he seemed. Maybe that was an illusion caused by his overzealousness. But even if he was smarter than that, it seemed unlikely that he could deal with the likes of Balu and Banerji on an even footing.

She lay back on the bed and looked through her kaleidoscope.

Max googled for photos of The Revolutionary Nuns on his phone and saw the faces of the roller derby team but armed and in starched military uniforms, expressionless, always flanking or just behind the immaculately dressed Colonel as he smiled or waved or both. Max kept swiping through them. The pictures made Robert Palmer look like a man in sweatpants at K-Mart with his mom's mahjong circle. When he looked up from his phone again, Tanuja was asleep.

7

1 purse containing $57.25 cash, car key, mobile phone, red cosmetic powder, kaleidoscope, family photo.
Personal effects inventory drawn up by Fredericton Police upon the arrest of Tanuja Ramachandran

Just as Pete Smith was drifting off to sleep, his assistant knocked on his bedroom door, and came in to tell him that Aaliyah was dead. The details were insane beyond belief. Smith tried desperately to force them out of his head, but his mind was screaming Aaliyah's name and face. Think of something else, he told himself…

Flat track. Get back out of bed. Mind festering, burning. *Legal Pass. Jam Start. Pivot.* Pick up yesterday's pants off the floor. Throw them down in rage. Pick them up again. Put them back on again. Cross the room. *Second pass. Passive offensive.* Open the closet. Look for a shirt. *Illegal procedure. Jammer lap point.* No, not that one. Find a cleaner shirt. Every one's got artwork by Ed

74

Repka blazoned on it. Visualize Aaliyah soaring around the track over and over again, pulling off apex jumps like she was born with wings, her helmet and pads gleaming under the arena lights. No more apex jumps, no more powerjams, no more body checks for Aaliyah. All the things that mattered, the only things that mattered, all gone.

Now, use your head. Come on. Call in some favors. Call the coroner on your cell phone. Get her out of bed. Try to steady your voice. Ten minutes later, she's there herself with the police to collect the body. She says something that sounds like: "There's nothing you can do. Stay here. I'll call you in the morning." At times like this, you're thankful for your parents' money at least. *Snowplow, grand slam, rink rash.* Stay awake all night with the women in the house angry and wailing, blaming you. Yes, you are to blame. It's the only aspect of the whole thing you can swallow. None of it adds up. Roller derby is the one thing that can ensure a healthy mind and body. So how can she be dead? Just last night, you were all soaring high on the win of the season. But now...

Finally, the phone call comes. Couldn't they just penalty kill her back to life? Some of the others insist on coming with you, to hear what happened. In your mind, you see Aaliyah do a Triple Salchow jump, like a figure skater, then skim across the track backwards with one leg up, back arched, like she's on a sheet of silver ice.

***

"She choked to death trying to eat a squirrel?!"

The still body of the woman was laid out flat on a stainless steel table in the morgue, its cold surface reflecting Pete Smith's saddened-now-confounded face back up at him as a Renoirian blur.

On the other side of the table across from him was the sympathetic Caucasian face of Jane West, the coroner Pete had woken up in the middle of the night. It was a testament to West's abilities that she'd been able to do her job, even in this makeshift facility.

At the foot of the table stood Greg Flynn, another Caucasian and the town sheriff. He still had his high school good looks, and the weight he'd put on just made him look more solid and adult. He had never intended to become a cop for life, but once he grew the moustache there was no turning back.

West frowned at Pete, but there was compassion in her voice. "I'm sorry, Pete. Accidental suicide."

Pete turned away from the body and massaged his temple, ran a hand over his face. Flynn, the sheriff, started nodding to himself as he took in what the coroner said and started to believe it. "No, I get it," he said. "It's a Muslim thing. They're vegetarian, right? One night she gets desperate for meat. Everybody does, it's our nature. So she goes out, frantic, tries to eat a live squirrel, gets more than she bargained for. Hitler went nuts the same way."

Pete turned around and eyed the sheriff. "Jesus Christ, Greg, Muslims aren't vegetarians." To West he said, "So what about Akmal?"

West shrugged. "That's not my department. Greg?"

"It's plain as day, Pete. Look: kid's up in the tree jerking off, loses his balance, falls, knocks himself out. Aaliyah hears the noise, comes over to investigate, gets distracted by the squirrel, Hitler."

Pete was slow to respond. He stared down at the body, cold, gray, and permanent. "Yeah," he ventured, "yeah, I guess so."

"I'm going to have to cut him loose, Pete," said Flynn. "Those two out-of-towners too."

Pete nodded at him, his mouth a straight line trying to keep any of the emotion from seeping out while his eyes welled up again.

***

There were seven other women in the temporary holding cell along with Tanuja, every class of criminal from tattooed local drag racing legends to two East German prostitutes – one that looked like a Fox anchorwoman, the other practically a Dolph Lundgren impersonator. They were all pressed up against the perimeter chanting and fist-pumping while Tanuja faced off against a tight-skirted investment banker in the center of the cell. The women in the adjoining cell chanted too, separated only by a barrier of bars. In one corner was a toilet that stank up the whole room and the seat of which – defying comprehension – was covered in piss. The concrete walls around the cells and through the hallway leading to them were painted a pale 80s yellow. The addition of lockers would have made it indistinguishable from Degrassi Junior High.

The banker was gaunt but hard, her hair tied in a bun threatening strand by strand to pop loose, her thigh-length skirt just lax enough to allow her to take a defensive stance against Tanuja. She had her fists up in a keen attack posture, but these were fists that had only been tempered against gropy office fuckwits on her way up to the top where she too could eat canapés off naked women with her lecherous male cohorts. Tanuja adjusted her sari and tried not to smirk.

The woman lunged and the audience's holler was instantaneous. Tanuja dodged with an easy shuffle to the right and slapped the Corporate Mama – *dishum!* – full on the left cheek. The woman didn't hesitate to throw a punch with her left, but it was even slower. Tanuja delivered another stinging slap – *dishum!* – this time to her right cheek. This time Executive Lady registered shock. Tanuja used the opportunity to administer three more: left, right, left – *dishum, dishum, dishum!* Flaming with rage, the woman threw again. Tanuja spun back on her heel to dodge the punch, grabbed the arm and extended it across her chest, and elbowed the suit in the tits. But they had the consistency of a memory foam pillow and the woman showed no sign of pain. The banker twisted and her free fist came at Tanuja's face. Tanuja ducked, dislocating the shoulder of the trapped arm – this time the woman screamed. Still low, Tanuja swept the woman's bare legs up off the ground and the back of her head hit the concrete. Tanuja elbow dropped her for good measure with an impact that could have liquefied her innards, but she was already unconscious.

The audience cheered and clapped. One of the women came over and gave Tanuja a twenty. A few others came over and patted her on the shoulders.

"Hey! Hey!" A cop with pasty white skin had appeared at the door and was rapping her billy club against the bars over the ruckus. "Which one of you is Ta– Ta–" She looked down at her clipboard and furrowed her brow.

The Dolph stood up and started walking towards the cell door. "Tammy Orloff. That's me," she said.

"All right." The cop unlocked the cell. "You're free to go," she said.

"Tammy" walked out the door and disappeared down the Degrassi corridor to Mr Raditch's class. The cop looked at her clipboard again. "Wait, no, no, that's not right." She looked down the hall, but Tammy was already gone. "Ta– Tanoo–" she started again.

"Tanuja Ramachandran."

"That's it. You're free to go."

***

Tanuja collected her things from the processing clerk. Everything from her purse had been taken out and individually bagged. The Caucasian processing clerk checked them off as he handed each one back to her. At the end of it, he looked at her to indicate he was done, but her eyes were fixed on another white cop a few meters away behind the counter, sitting with her legs up on a desk and squinting through a little kaleidoscope. The processing clerk followed her gaze. Tanuja cleared her throat and the seated cop stopped playing long enough to notice Tanuja's iron stare. With an embarrassed frown, she walked over with the kaleidoscope and handed it to her. The processing clerk looked down at his list and checked it off.

Tanuja was putting on her earrings as she entered the front reception area. She found Max on a bench there against the wall, his shirt torn and dirtied, a large bruise on his temple. He was too defeated even to stand up when she came up to him, but he sang: "*Spent the night in jail! Had to pee into a pail!*" He looked at her in mild bemusement.

Standing in front of him, she said, "You look like you just lost twenty bucks."

"How did you know?!"

"Lucky guess."

He looked her up and down then shrank back in dejected self-pity. "I can't believe those cops gave you all that time to get changed at the motel before they dragged us down here."

"I convinced them not to bother searching our room too," she said. "If only you'd been born a woman, all these powers could be yours too, Maximum Pervert."

"All right already! Did they ever tell you what they were holding you for?"

Tanuja shook her head.

"Me neither."

"There's only one thing it could have been."

"The roller skater."

She nodded. "They didn't want us skipping town, just in case. I don't think we're in the clear yet, but it's obvious they've got nothing."

Max mustered the strength to wrench himself up from the bench. Tanuja clasped his elbow to help, and they made their way towards the glass exit doors.

When they pushed through the second set of doors and into the noonday sun, the light blinded them, but they could hear some sort of altercation happening on the opposite side of the street. A second later when their eyes adjusted, from their elevated position on the police station steps, they saw that it was Pete Smith, three of the Qarnage Queens, and a young brown man with greasy hair in a leather jacket and jeans. The brown man had taken a few punches in the face: swollen cheek, split, bleeding lip. The women were furious. Pete was trying to hold them back from the brown man, and shield him at the same time to keep them from hitting him again. Their bloodlust was already subsiding, but they were all streaming tears through gritted teeth, and one of the women crouched into a weeping ball right there on the sidewalk. Off to one side, a man who seemed to be the town sheriff was looking on with only passing interest. None of his business apparently.

"Hey, I know that guy," Max said. "He was in the cell with me."

"He's the Jerk Off," Tanuja answered.

"The what?"

"From last night."

She put her hand on Max's back and led him back through the outer double doors to avoid being seen, and then pressed him against the wall. She did the same. Out on the street Pete raised the crouching woman up and hugged her. The other women clustered around them. Akmal stayed where he was and sulked at the pavement, the bushes, the weather. Sheriff Greg Flynn shifted like a statue struggling to come to life.

Smith's SUV was parked near the scene. He opened the back door for the women and they filed in. Then he went around back and popped the back open. He pulled out what looked like three large cans of paint. Akmal walked over and took them from him at arm's length, his nose curling as if some serious stink was coming from the cans. Pete directed some stern words to him, then got in the car himself and drove off. Akmal watched them for a minute, then turned and started walking in the opposite direction.

Tanuja turned to Max and said, "Something weird is going on. Walk back to the motel and get the Charger. I'll follow Whack-Off Smirnov. Make sure you bring my Roknas."

Max nodded and went out in the same general direction that the SUV had gone. Tanuja started down the steps after Akmal, but the sheriff was crossing the street right in front of her, waving at her. "Hold on there a second, ma'am!" he called out. She stopped two steps up, looking down at him.

"I'd, uh, I'd like to apologize for your getting locked up like that. There was, there was an incident last night."

"And me being an out-of-towner, you assumed I was responsible," she said scowling down. "What was it? A break-in? A bank-robbery"

"Look, I'm sorry," he said. He realized himself that his apology was starting to sound defensive, when something occurred to him and he switched tack. "Fredericton is perfectly safe, but *stay safe* while you're here. There's been… there's been some things going on in this town the past year or so…" He trailed off in thought, pressed his lips together, and started walking past her up the stairs.

Tanuja grabbed his arm and held him before he could pass. "What kind of things?" she asked.

"There've been four disappearances in fourteen months," he said. His eyes betrayed him by adding, *That we know of.* "It's been in the news some. You might have heard about it." She hadn't heard about it. Even Shastri must have known nothing of it, since she hadn't mentioned it in the briefing. When she said nothing, he continued. "Mostly homeless types. We've been doing everything in our power, but…" The remorse in his voice was obvious. "Don't get into any trouble. And don't go in the woods."

"The woods?" she asked with arched brow.

"Bobcat trouble, we think. And don't go in the river."

She only stared at him.

"… Beavers," he said.

The ineffectuality of all his warnings expressed itself as shame in his eyes. The look made her let go of him, this big man transformed into a helpless child by guilt. *What the fuck was going on in this town?* she thought.

She watched the sheriff's receding back for a moment then went down the steps after Akmal.

***

Aaliyah had gone shooting clear off the track of life, smashed right into the bleachers and was out of the game. For good. For a moment, Pete Smith wondered if he had failed her as a coach, but what Aaliyah had done was insane beyond anything he could be held responsible for. If anything, it was "manufacturer error," as if a wheel had popped off of one of her skates.

The night had helped to numb the shock, but driving still required tremendous focus. The reality of it was that he hardly knew Aaliyah. No, the problem was that things were getting weird with the team and he felt, in some way that he couldn't articulate, that the team was turning into something beyond him. The death of Aaliyah was the ultimate confirmation of it. And the grief of the other women was going to make things worse. Unconsciously, Pete had hoped the motion of driving would ease the women's pain, like rocking a baby, as he drove them back home after leaving the station.

As the world outside the SUV slid past the window frames like so much ephemera, everyone inside the car felt the transience of existence. One of their sisters was dead. And yet Pete could sense in their chilly silence that, for some of them, their sadness had mutated within instants of it gripping them, like a block of ice starting to melt into vapor and coalescing again into something else before it could dissipate. Anger. The transition had happened sooner than he expected. It had to be *the treatment,* Pete realized. In a way, this was the very point of the treatment, it was supposed to change them like this, but seeing it in actual effect like this chilled him.

Jasmina in the back right passenger seat had been weeping openly on the street, and now she was singing to herself almost under her breath as though she was forcing herself to do it. But Pete could sense it was not an act of self-comfort. It was a war chant, one sung in a desperate, husky voice. She was wearing a thin headscarf in a bright green and blue floral pattern.

Zilal in the passenger seat behind him was the

hardest to read. She was too quiet. Her composure was icy. Beside him in the front, Flora gazed out her window, tears trickling in a lightning zigzag down over her clenched jaw. Her head nearly touched the ceiling.

Jasmina's singing was starting to make him nuts, so he switched on the stereo, and they got through about three bars of "N.I.B." with him wailing along before Flora punched the radio panel like a Mack truck. Her fist seemed to come away from it in slow motion, revealing a sparking, wiry paste where the dials used to be.

"Jesus Christ!" Pete cried. "Do you realize how much it's going to cost me to replace that 8-track player?!" But when he saw Flora's glare, he immediately backpedaled. "Uh, never mind," he said. He was angry about Aaliyah not the stereo anyway.

The outburst of violence had shaken Jasmina from her daze. "Wh-what happened…?" she stammered from the back seat.

Flora scoffed out the window. The sound had a lethal quality to it. "So that's it," she said as if to the universe. It was delivered as a tautology, not a question. "Akmal gets a slap on the wrist. And that woman in the sari walks away. No suspects."

"Woman in the sari?" Jasmina asked. Zilal was still gazing out the window, absent.

"Pete's new sweetheart," Flora jeered.

"You mean the woman that was outside the police station?" Jasmina said. The question didn't need to be answered. Pete looked out his window at all of life's skaters out there on the sidewalks, getting checked and passed and probably losing the game. His mind called up the image of Tanuja's face, her almond eyes, her *gulab jamun* lips… In his reverie, the SUV started listing to the right, and he didn't right himself until a woman pushing a baby carriage screamed and fled from his accidental lime green rampage.

"It's funny," Jasmina said. "You know, I saw a woman in a sari in the parking lot last night before the match. She was talking to Wood."

"What?!" That got all of their attention.

"She was talking with Sue Wood?" Pete repeated. The roller derby talk had brought his awareness back into razor sharp focus. "Did you hear what they said?"

"No. I don't know. Wood seemed angry. That's all."

"Pete!" Flora cried. "Fuck!"

"No, no!" Pete protested. "I mean, Sue's a cheating cheater, but she wouldn't put out a hit on one of ours just to gain an advantage for her own team, right? Hell, we don't even know that it was the same woman in the first place. I mean, right?"

Zilal finally spoke. "I – I agree with Pete. It would be insane."

Flora ignored her. "I don't know, Pete. If it meant winning their precious roller derby, I know some people who would go much, much further even." They locked eyes and he was entangled until another pedestrian screamed at the SUV bearing down on him.

He mustered up the strength to challenge her. "Hey, this," – he made a circling motion with his index finger to indicate everyone in their sphere – "this isn't cheating. Steroids is cheating. There's nothing in any of the rules about pheromone treatment. We're all on board with this. You guys wanted it just as bad, uh, remember? You were, you were into the idea even before I was." Even in the autumn chill, a trickle of sweat travelled down one of his sideburns. He was in such close striking distance of all of them.

Flora arched an incredulous eyebrow. "And this all makes Sue Wood innocent how?"

"Aw, goddamn it!" he shouted while pounding the steering wheel.

"No, Pete," Zilal said from behind him, "it must be a coincidence. Sue Wood is just some schlub. She wouldn't be capable."

Pete had a focused look on his face. He had a firm grip on the wheel, but it was obvious to everyone in the car that he was replaying the conversation they'd just had in his mind again word by word.

"Are you even going to cancel that soiree you have planned for tomorrow?" Flora asked.

"I can't," he muttered. "I got a call last night. There's going to be a special guest. If anything, it's going to be more people." They'd have to amp up the security too.

Flora said nothing.

He turned a hard left.

"Hey, where are we going?" Jasmina asked. "Aren't we going home?"

"Look, tensions are a bit high, which is to be expected of course," Pete said. "But there is a solution. The only thing that's going to make us feel any better. Might I suggest that we all get our skates on and have a practice? Can we? Please?"

Jasmina slumped into her seat and started weeping again. Zilal stared at the floor wide-eyed. Flora scoffed out the window again and the sound was like a machete cutting off a tiger's head.

8

*There is a tale in the Mahabharata in which the
great teacher Dronacharya instructed his students
to aim their bows at a bird in a tree at great
distance. To each student in turn he asked,
"What do you see?" The first said, "The sky, the
tree, the bird." Drona dismissed him. The second
said, "I see only the bird." Drona dismissed him.
Arjuna said, "I see only the eye of the bird."
Drona allowed him to fire, and Arjuna's arrow
struck true. Now, let me tell you: Tanuja
Ramachandran sees only the eyes of birds, and she
sees them everywhere.*

Govinda Banerji, intercepted communication

Akmal started off towards the main downtown area in
front of the riverbank, but before reaching it, he turned
onto a side street, and then into a narrow alleyway
between two strips of shops. Tanuja kept her distance.
From the street where he entered the alley, she did not
get to see the fronts of the shops – she had no idea what

they were from here. She saw him fish out some keys, open the back door to a two-story building, and go in. She circled around to the front of the street, then crossed to the opposite side so she could see the whole strip of shops and work out which one Akmal had gone into. It had a faux deco façade that made it look like something out of the 20s, and there was a big painted sign up over the second story that revealed it to be the Fredericton Smell-O-Vision Cinema. It was next door to the diner they'd been at the night before. The sign made the building look even more overpowering compared to the shops that flanked it on either side.

She returned to her vantage of the alley again and waited. After about five minutes, Akmal came out through the same door and threw the three cans into a dumpster in the alley. Then he walked back out the alley and went right past Tanuja without noticing her, looking at the ground with fervent shame the whole time.

Tanuja watched him go, then went to the dumpster. It was easy enough to reach one of the cans. She pulled it out and sniffed it. The smell almost made her retch. But it wasn't paint. She didn't know what it was, it reeked of a million things: sweat and cheese and roses and belches. She tried another can and it was a separate set of stenches: phlegm, rotten meat, wet fur, and beach toilets.

She was about to throw this one back too, when suddenly there was a hulking homeless man beside her and she could sense the tension of his muscles underneath his rags. He was in a bad way.

"Hey, you, you lard-ass, thass, thass *my* fucking stink!" he pointed and threatened. When he spoke his lower jaw swung in loose, mad, Grunge rock yarls, like it was completely unhinged from the rest of his skull.

The can still in her hand, Tanuja retreated a step and her years of exacting *prana-bindu* training took over her body, every muscle and nerve instantly at maximum alertness. The dumpster lid slammed shut with a devastating clang.

"Bolo! Wait!" a voice called out from behind the yarler. A figure stepped out of the shadows and stopped next to the big man. This one was shorter but looked just as rough. He was wearing a rat-chewed trench coat that must have been sweltering and an Edmonton Oilers toque, but he had a composed quality that suggested he had his wits about him. "I suggest you give him his stink, young lady. He's not very nice without it."

Tanuja looked at the can in her hand and handed it to the big oaf. His tongue shot out like a cartoon character and he cradled the can like it was a puppy. Then he retreated to a grimy brick wall, where he sat on the ground and proceeded to lick the innards of his precious can of "stink."

"How can he stand it?" Tanuja asked the toque-wearing man in disgust.

"He cannot live without it. Bolo is homeless, a

beggar, a panhandler, a street dweller, a bum, a hobo, a vagrant, a drifter, a vagabond, a tramp, a dumpster diver, a man of the rails –"

"I get the picture."

"– as am I. All he has is his stink. You do not belong here, madam. I can see it in the eyes of you."

"I'll be out of your alley in a minute, rail rider."

"You may call me… Oilers Toque Man. And I meant you do not belong *in this town*, madam. Best leave before you become… part of something else." He collected his big, stink-eating friend Bolo and left the alley.

Tanuja didn't bother to go back into the dumpster to smell the third can.

Baffled, she exited the alley and fished out her phone and called Max.

"Max," she said, "I followed the guy, and I've got *something*. It may be a lead. I don't know, but it's weird. I want you to come watch a movie with me."

"We just got out of jail, and you want to go to the movies?!"

"And bring my Roknas with you. I'm standing right in the middle of Queen Street," she said looking at the sign. "You'll see me."

Fifteen minutes later Max pulled up and parked in front of her and they went into the Fredericton Smell-O-Vision Cinema together to watch *Silent Running*.

***

The theater only had one screen. There were about fifteen other people in there besides Tanuja and Max – a phenomenal number for a weekday matinee of a 40-year-old science fiction movie, she guessed. Tanuja had never even heard of this movie about space gardens and robots and Bruce Dern, but she figured it could be Pete Smith's cup of tea. Watching it, she found Bruce Dern more handsome than she'd have expected. He had a kind of controlled virility about him, it was smoldering beneath his skin, like a phantasmal shadow that was his to command. And there he was, out there on that space station in the cold of outer space, with his plants and his robots.

Then a few minutes into the movie, something strange happened. She *smelled* him. She could smell Bruce Dern in the cinema, and his ferns, and the steel. It was such a strange, artificial experience. Smell-O-Vision had been an occasional and ultimately unsuccessful gimmick in the fifties. What could have possessed anyone to revive it here and now?

Max smelled it too, and leaped up. "Gas attack!" he yelped. Some of the other patrons gave him annoyed looks and grumbles, some chuckles.

Tanuja grabbed his arm and pulled him back down. "No wait," she said. Everyone else in the cinema was intent on the screen again. When Bruce went to his cabin to sleep, the smells changed. Clean sheets, detergent, disinfectant. Tanuja started to understand it. It was a crude gimmick, but the effect wasn't overwhelming. They had executed it with some restraint, and it wasn't applied to every scene of the movie. When the smell got switched on it was an unexpected surprise every time. She caught herself uncrossing and crossing her legs whenever Dern was on screen at the same time as the smell, and had to make a conscious effort to stop it. She fell asleep twice during the screening, but only for about five minutes each time.

When the show ended, Tanuja and Max shuffled out with the crowd into the lobby which smelled of popcorn and also a faint mix of all those other things which had become embedded into the carpet and wood after hundreds of screenings. Nobody noticed that she still smelled like jail. As the rest of the audience started to exit to the street, Tanuja and Max went back to see the pimply-faced, pallid white sixteen-year-old who'd sold them their ticket at the concession counter. Her haircut was a Heidi of the Alps copyright infringement of the highest order.

She looked up at them as they approached. "Welcome to Smell-O-Vision Cinema – Atlantic Canada's only Smell-O-Vision, and the number one tourist attraction in Fredericton! Tickets for the 12:00 show?" she asked.

"We just bought tickets to see the *last* show, remember?"

The kid snickered. "Oh, right! Of course. Sorry. Short attention span. Well, what can I do for you?"

"Pete Smith owns this place?" Tanuja asked.

The kid snickered again. "What *doesn't* he own in this burg!"

"What's the deal with the smells?"

"Well, it's some sorta mix of chemicals." Tanuja could see her brain struggling to remember the script. "During the show, the projectionist has to, like, pour in other chemicals in perfect amounts by hand to create certain smells, and then he pumps them through the filters on cue. Would you like a flyer?"

"Already got one," Tanuja said holding up the one she'd picked up two hours earlier. "Do you know where they make the stuff?"

The teen stared saucer-eyed for a moment, then said in a quavering voice: "Well, it's a mix of chemicals. During the show, the projectionist has to pour in other chemicals by hand to create certain smells and pump them through the filters on cue. Would you like a flyer?"

Someone who'd been in the audience walked past and waved at the ticket seller. The teen waved back, obviously glad of the interruption.

Tanuja turned and went out into the street with Max following and once again they were squinting under the glare of the sun.

Out on the side walk, she said, "So what the fuck was that about?"

"Which part of it?"

"Any of it! The smells first of all."

"Was it… mind control?"

She furrowed her brow in disbelief. "To what effect? Do you feel any different?"

"No," he admitted after a long pause.

"So what were all those people doing in there?"

Max thought for a second. "Tourists?" he ventured.

"Maybe. But that kid working the box office waved at that guy like he was a regular."

"Okay, so… the smell stuff has some sort of… addictive property."

She looked down at the pavement for an instant. "What did you think of the movie?" she asked him.

His eyes lit up. "I loved it!"

Tanuja nodded. "So did I. Do you feel like you want to see it again?"

The grin never left his face. "Yeah! Absolutely!"

"Me too now that I think about it. Maybe there's something there," she thought aloud.

She looked hard in Max's face. The grin had faded. He was looking off down the street, avoiding eye contact. "What is it?" she said.

"I… uh… uh…," he stuttered. "*We watched a movie! Its hours were less than three!*"

"Say it!" she cried, headlocking him in the street.

"I… I got a boner in there," he managed to squeak.

Her eyes widened. She turned around and marched back through the cinema doors with Max nearly stumbling after her to keep up.

When the ticket kid saw them approach, she started to say, "Welcome to Smell-O-Vision Cinema –

Atlantic Canada's only Smell-O-Vision, and the number one tourist attr—" but Tanuja had marched in a straight line towards her, flipped up the barrier, crossed to her side of the counter, and slammed her down bent over backwards against it with her forearm against her neck. Max watched the scene from a distance in silent alarm.

"Where's the projectionist?" she asked.

"Th-through that door there over by the toilets, th-then up the stairs," she stammered.

Tanuja released her grip on her but the red stare of her *pottu* kept her pinned to the spot gazing up at her in terror. She reached into the display case beside her, and came up with a Mr Big chocolate bar. "I'm taking this," she declared.

The teen nodded with autonomic enthusiasm. Tanuja backed away and nodded to Max to come over. The ticket kid was recovering but went into a cowering defensive posture as Max approached.

Max glared at the Mr Big bar in Tanuja's hand. "After making us sit through all those commercials," she said, "they should be paying *me* to eat their candy."

She broke off half for him. "Stay here and watch the kid. Make sure she doesn't call the cops." Max nodded and watched her go through the door and up a white stairwell.

At the top of the stairs the smells were more obvious. The landing was a small alcove, and across from the steps was a door – obviously the projection room. Tanuja opened the door and waltzed right in.

The projectionist was in his fifties, heavy and sweating and underdressed with patchy white skin. He was completely mismatched: a diamond-etched face on top of a putty body. When Tanuja burst in, he was adjusting some equipment but swiveled and stood up to face her. "Hey, you can't be in here!" he barked. His voice was wet and gross.

"*Dey*! Who makes the stuff?" Tanuja demanded.

The projectionist was infuriated. "Hey, fuck you!"

Tanuja punched him in the solar plexus and he half landed on a rotating stool that carried him careening half way to the wall on its casters before dumping him on the ground and itself tipping over with an ill-mannered clatter.

He struggled through the ringing in his head to right himself into a sitting position only to find the barrel of a Roknas looking down at him. He raised his hands without even thinking about it.

"Who makes it?" Tanuja asked again.

"How should I know? Hell, you're one of Pete's ladies, ain'tcha – *you* tell *me*."

Against her will, Tanuja's eyelids became heavy and an instant later, much to the projectionist's surprise, she began listing to her left, then nodded off in an upright position propped against a crook in the wall.

"She… she must be some kinda retard!" the projectionist whispered to himself. He wrenched himself up and started to inch forward, arms forward and fingers wriggling in anticipation of wringing her neck.

She bolted awake and her arm sprung out and clutched his throat. Just behind her, there was a cluster of large, pressure-sealed stainless steel drums connected to the equipment. Tanuja popped the latched lid on one and it opened with a hiss. The smell was unforgiving.

"What are you –" the projectionist started to ask, but even through the blur of motion he already knew. He was swept sideways, as though he'd been lifted by a giant bat, and then in a sudden downwards arc as his head went into the soup.

She gave him a few seconds under then yanked him out and his head was covered in a thick pink slime. He slumped back to the floor exactly where he'd been before, only now he looked like he'd just spent a month on "You Can't Do That On Television" during Pepto Bismol season.

"I – I don't remember his name, okay?" he stammered. "I only met him once. He showed me how to work the dials, I never saw him again. He was a Paki like you. Seemed like a nice enough guy." She kicked him in the nuts and he howled.

"Where do they make the smells?" she asked, and the gun barrel fluttered ever so slightly between his eyes, a black hole that would stretch him like taffy into infinity once he teetered over its event horizon. "There must be a production lab somewhere. Tell me."

"They don't tell me. Some camel jockey always drops it off. I – what are you doing?"

Tanuja had backed across the room towards the door to get enough room for a run up. Realization started to dawn on him. "No – no, wait! Listen, wait for the delivery truck! You'll see," he spluttered, "Lots more than just candy bars, but this is never where – aaaahhh!!"

Tanuja flew at him with the dexterity of a Bharanatyam dancer, and landed a twin-footed kick in his face that cracked his head against the wall and knocked him out. It was spectacular overkill, but worth the effort, and easy enough for her since she'd practiced it hundreds of times on Max when they were kids before and even *during* their time at the orphanage. She rolled herself up off the ground with a half laugh / half groan and looked at her handiwork. "Classic!" the Rani said with a clap and a smile.

Max's voice projected from the doorway. "*Aiyyoyo!*" he cried. "What the fuck happened up here?! It smells like *amma*'s masala!"

"I thought I told you to stay downstairs!"

"I slipped the kid a fifty. She's happy as a clam. What about this guy?"

"It doesn't matter," she said zipping her heat back into her purse. "He thinks I'm one of the Queens." But she froze and stared at the unconscious hill of meat against the wall. She thought, remembered what Max had said outside, thought about the pink goo all over the projectionist's head, and then wrenched his pants down to his ankles.

"Again?" Max squawked.

"Sometimes," she replied, "any problem can be solved by pulling down a man's pants."

9

Strength does not come from physical capacity. It comes from an indomitable will.
Mahatma Gandhi, 1920

Srikanth Balu looked down the rows of desperate, mostly homeless men and women in cages to either side of him and wondered, *Whatever happened to Ace of Bass?*

On another track in his mind (he could process as many as four things at once unless *it* came up), he was dismantling and recombining a series of molecules trying to work out the configuration that would produce the right physiological effect.

And then there was the deep, red angry line that coursed through his consciousness. It was Srikanth Balu's unwavering awareness that his life was garbage.

He still had his looks. He was under forty with fine brushed hair, keen eyes, and a pointed chin. In less stressful circumstances he might have passed for a jocular uncle.

More importantly, he was the greatest scientific mind of his generation. He had two PhDs from Annamalai University, and had graduated at 22. In fact, he had earned the highest distinctions in the university's history and twenty years later, they were still untouched. But his work since was so good that it was almost entirely illegal. The typical shackles of all true geniuses: the civilizations they existed in were too far behind them, and were so shamed and frightened that they relegated these monumental intellects to the fringes. Even when he had done work for the government – as early as age 17 – it was all off the books, and was so potentially scandalous to the big shots that commissioned it that they usually wanted him dead afterwards. And so he was nearly always on the run, and now here he was in butt-fuck Canada working for this man-child Pete Smith with his devil-worshipping head banger music. And so rich this man was, but always in t-shirts – his stupid noisy music t-shirts! And his stupid roller derby and his jazz cigarettes! It was insufferable. *Why didn't anyone care about Bros anymore?!* Balu's mind raged. He had once tried to compose a compound that could correct cultural taste, but the psychological barriers were too strong. It had proved impossible… so far.

Well, this Pete was made of money at least, and was happy to spend it on his ridiculous science projects. And the other good thing was that Pete was so stupid he'd never know what his money was really being lavished on. But it infuriated Balu that he still had to waste his time with such business. He was thirty-six-years old! Shouldn't a man with a mind like his be allowed to do what he wanted with his time by now?! Hadn't he paid his dues and earned his stripes?

There were five cages on each side. The aisle between them was wide enough so he could push his trolley of equipment through when he needed it. Behind him was the way to the main lab: a door with a prominent "No Entry" sign on the other side of it. Pete Smith was stupid enough to respect it. "Highly sensitive work. Contamination would be catastrophic," Balu had told him. There was also a heavy steel door at the other end of the lab leading to the outdoors. Balu had sleeping quarters down here too, and they were wretched.

The cages were all equally as roomy as the aisle for the same reason, and they were a clean laboratory white. Most of their occupants were haggard and listless, lounging around their cells with slumped shoulders in their hospital gowns. Few of them bothered to look up when he came in. Those that did showed no emotion. Some of the more *advanced* ones paced their cells with a curious, animalistic quality. Balu had improved them. If not them personally, then their species. Some of them though…

The heavy steel door at the end of the aisle swung open on noisy hinges, revealing a dark tunnel on the other side that was in stark contrast to the antiseptic quality surrounding Balu. Two of Gaddafi's Virgins came through hauling a large body bag with relative ease. *Those hinges will have to be looked at before all that noise back here raises suspicions*, he thought.

"What took you so long?" he growled, immediately regretting his tone of voice. He had almost barked when the door opened, but seeing these two – practically a Valkyrie on one side, and a gladiator on the other – he trembled inside. "Smith will be here for the evening package any minute now if he keeps to his schedule." Balu's voice was barely more than a mutter.

They walked right up to his end of the aisle, and dumped the body in front of him. They never answered his question or betrayed any sign of respect for his profession. *Yes, of course*, he remembered, *Smith lost his "best jammer" last night.*

Balu looked at the two women. Just this morning, they too had learned that one of their own had died. Was the desire for revenge, revenge against all squirrels, festering behind those killer eyes? They were unreadable, especially now that they'd had so much of the treatment. And knowing Pete Smith, he would probably make them keep going to roller derby practice as usual anyway.

The one on his left looked like a five-foot tall pro wrestler who'd been assigned a librarian persona. The one on the right was tall, mouth always slightly open and suggestive, and she was decked out like Imelda Marcos. Her earrings and lip gloss were so blinding,

Balu had to wince and squint just to look at her. She was wearing enormous Dolce & Gabbana sunglasses with "D" and "G" in big diamond studded block letters on each arm. They looked like they'd been designed by a five-year old. This one – Safeera, a.k.a. Saucy Safeera – amazed him to no end. Had she really gone out into the streets to abduct a homeless man dressed like this? He stole a glance at her shoes. Four-inch stiletto heels. It was unbelievable.

"Okay, let me see it," he said. Safeera knelt down to unzip the bag, and he had a good view of her prominent cleavage. For a moment, the chemical compound he was considering and all thoughts of "Rico Suave" left his mind. That was *it*. All thoughts derailed for tits or ass. When she got up again, he continued to stare at the unconscious homeless man in the bag in order to re-align his thoughts. This too incensed him. How much time did men waste every hour thinking about sex? Every *minute*? It was outrageous. Whoever the idiot was who invented Viagra had it all wrong. Balu called up in his mind a molecule that he had been working on that would suppress sexual drive while leaving aggression unaffected – both regulated by testosterone. He'd never been able to work out the right arrangement, but think of the increase in productivity! Across the entire world!

On an alternate track, his mind pondered the fact of his line of sight darting to her breasts in an autonomic manner. It was a physiological reaction. Of course it was. The cleavage of the rear end is the primary sex characteristic for mammals that walk on all fours: it triggers a chemical attraction in the males. When humans began to walk upright, cleavage on chests evolved as a new eye-level substitute. It was only natural for Balu's body to react as it did, without thought. Every species in existence past, present, and future was a DNA delivery mechanism built to propagate and no more. All else was the interference of civilization. But the waste of it…!

He started to run through re-sequencings of gene patterns in his head to select out attraction to large breasts. It would take work, maybe even years, but eventually he might hit on it. He filed it away. Of course, sometimes a significant enough cultural force could mask physiological imperatives… the fashion of small breasts in South America… but such trends were fickle and temporary. Within one to two hundred years, biology would overcome again, as it always did.

That made him think of male subjugation of women too. This too was culture attempting to suppress biology. An unspoken and unconscious social contract between the males of our species to maintain a position of superiority over the female gender and force them into a position in which they would be less able to refuse sex. *Well, not for much longer*, he thought looking again at the two women in front of him. *Not by the time I'm done with them.* Suppressing the male sex drive would solve the problem, but he couldn't work out the formula for that yet. But this was another solution. Sometimes, he knew, nature needed a helping hand regaining its dominance.

"Did you say something?" the librarian said. He remembered her name now: Jaiyana. She was like a coiled spring. Balu thought she might slug him with a hardcover copy of *Ulysses* at any given moment.

"… What…?" he said. He had been lost in thought for all of seven seconds.

"It sounded like you said something."

"Mm. No. Was just thinking," he covered. If he was starting to mumble unconsciously, he would have to watch out for that.

"Well?" Safeera deigned to ask him. Her glistening lips were still slightly parted in that way.

Balu looked down at the man again. The face reminded him of someone. Who…? Was it that heroin addict singer from the 90s that ruined music forever and then killed himself? A surge of rage coursed through his entire body and then subsided.

"He'll do," he finally answered. "Safeera." He thought for a moment and then nodded at one of the cages. "Number seven."

Her heels clip-clopped as she went over to the cell, unlocked it with a key from her pocket, and led out the near catatonic inmate. Again, Balu was astonished and frightened. She had not hesitated in the slightest. They never did. She would take that man out to the semicircle of woods at the rear of the property, shoot him dead with no compunction whatsoever, and take care of the body as he instructed. He could understand the reluctant need to do such things for the sake of science, but these women… it was like a bloodlust in them! Where had Banerji ever found them?! No, he knew where he had found them. They were Gaddafi's orphans, of course, but… to think how much worse they would be *afterwards*… The necessity of it weighed on him, but he was almost appalled.

Safeera took the inmate from number seven out through the door into the dark tunnel she'd come in from. Jaiyana dragged the new arrival into the empty cell behind her, one-handed.

The phone in his pocket vibrated. Would it never end!

No caller ID.

"Hello?"

"Srikanth."

Balu froze. "Banerji?" he asked. "Where are you? The reception's not so clear."

"On a plane, on my way to you. You-know-who has just announced a surprise visit to Fredericton. It's perfect. The entire schedule is accelerated. Gaddafi's Nuns can be the ones to carry it out." Despite the seeming urgency, Banerji had an unconcerned way of speaking. He was like a circling bird of prey. Conversation was an afterthought. In Balu's mind, Smith was an idiot, and Banerji was full of himself.

"What happened to the men I sent you? They needed six months of conditioning!"

"They're dead. And they weren't good enough, Srikanth. I need the next generation, especially for this. There's no time for field tests. It will be straight to the battlefield with them."

"We must make time for a test," Balu said, "The science demands it. But when exactly is all this happening?"

"The day after tomorrow. But…" He paused in his speech, like he was waiting to pounce. "There's something you should know. Tanuja Ramachandran will be on her way there too. Maybe she's there already."

"Who?"

"Srikanth. How could you not know? She's the one who murdered your little 'pet' back in 2001."

There was a long pause while Balu pursed his lips and processed.

"What's wrong, Srikanth?" Banerji asked. "I thought you'd be livid, hysterical for revenge."

"Oh, oh, yes, of course, revenge," Balu said slowly, but his mind was elsewhere. It was the word "murdered" that had derailed his thoughts.

"She wiped out the men you sent me. I almost had the chance to kill her, but sirens in the distance and all, you know?" Balu could almost hear the man shifting his wings and smoothing his feathers. "You might want to deal with her. She'll be at the worst motel in town. You'll love her, Balu. She's the kind of specimen you dream about – a complete neurotic. Obsessed with bizarre ancient swords and Scandinavian firearms. Anyway, as I said, I'm on my way. I'll call you in the morning."

"I understand," Balu said.

They said their goodbyes and Balu slid his phone back into his pocket. He thought for a second and then headed out the back door of the lab, through the dark tunnel to a short stairway that led up to an overhead hatch. He hurried through it and came out in the middle of a wide trail in the woods behind the mansion. The trees were frosted by moonlight, and there were tire tracks in the dirt. In the distance, he could see the lights of the mansion through the foliage. From here it looked like an exquisite dollhouse.

Safeera was up ahead in her Dolce & Gabbana sunglasses, with her gun pointed at the head of her prey on the ground. She turned when she heard the hatch drop shut.

"Safeera, wait!" Balu called out. Then he saw the wisp of smoke coming from the gun barrel and realized she'd already done it. How long had it taken her? Two, three minutes?

No matter now. "I need you to bring the, the body. Follow me," he said.

She picked the corpse up by one leg and dragged it behind her. Balu went off-trail, into the woods, and Safeera followed making so much noise hauling her load it was like a bulldozer snapping through the brush. She didn't seem to care about ruining her leather pants, though they must have cost $600, he guessed. She had her priorities in order, but after a few minutes she had to ask, "Where are we going?" It was only the second time she had condescended to speak to him tonight. "We don't want to stay out here too long. There are bobcats in these woods."

He looked at her and was at a loss for words, distracted by the moon reflecting off her wet lips. "There is no bobcat in these woods," was all he replied.

They pushed through another hundred meters or so, and then he entered the edge of a broad, dark, circular clearing that was obviously man-made. The moon had dipped behind a thin layer of clouds. They could barely see anything, but at the far end of the circle, Safeera thought she could make out the vague outline of what appeared to be a small, shoddy wooden shed. And, as her eyes adjusted… bones. Bones and skulls littered on the ground like the ruins of an ossuary.

In a hushed voice, Balu said, "Take it into the middle and leave it there."

She looked at him curiously, but didn't protest. She dragged the body over and let it slump there.

"Come back! Come back!" he whispered.

She joined him at the edge of the circle again. He touched her shoulder indicating they should crouch. "You're part of an elite club now, Safeera. You should feel privileged. Very few of you women get to feed my baby." Safeera had heard rumors of the thing. She'd never seen it.

Balu gave a low whistle and a *pss pss* noise like he was summoning a cat.

A sandy, shuffling noise came from the shed. And then a black shape loped out of it accompanied by the chunky rattle of a heavy chain with each broad step. Saucy Safeera recoiled, but Balu gripped her forearm to calm her. The thing circled around the body. She could tell now that its overall shape was vaguely humanoid: two arms, two legs, a head, though it looked smaller than a man. And the "arms" were long, almost touching the ground, and fingernails scraped the dirt with a sharp… metallic sound? It had an awkward, creeping gait, almost slithering, but as the moonlight improved, the incredible killing power in the muscles of the legs became obvious. Balu looked over at Safeera and saw her warrior muscles had instinctively tensed at the sight of the thing.

At last it started to edge towards the body, its coppery breathing hoarse and aroused, its downy chest swelling as it inhaled. As it came even closer, Safeera could now see that the oddly shaped head was actually a helmet: absinthe green, shimmering.

Balu smiled for the first time all night. "My baby boy…" he muttered, smiling. Safeera turned her face away in horror. The animal started eating the face off the corpse in the dirt, wrenched an arm off like a chicken leg and sucked the blood off the bone like it was a straw.

10

With each application of the treatment, the subjects display increasing refinement, exactly as I had predicted. How far I have come since those halcyon days of 1999! To think that these disgusting street people and these kamnaati barbarian roller skaters would make decent test subjects. And yet, my gradual conquest of their stubborn natures only serves as further proof of my unbounded intellect. Who'd have thought — ah! We could be lovers! She makes the bed! And he steals the covers!
Srikanth Balu, project notes

Here's how it went wrong for Max.

Meaning not necessarily in his life, but that evening. As for his life and how he'd ended up sniffing bicycle seats, he'd always blamed the shame of that scandal on the social maladjustment that came from his foster parents bringing him all the way to Canada and then teaching him nothing about sexual culture there. Not that they knew anything to teach him themselves. Meanwhile, Tanuja had not gone to England until she was in her teens. Although he wondered if, even so, perhaps she hadn't turned out even worse, sexually.

No, but that afternoon she told him to "get lost" while she waited in the alley behind the cinema for the delivery truck. He went to a museum and saw a fifty-pound frog from the 1880s that had been poorly taxidermied and looked like it had been fashioned out of papier-mache by an invalid. Then he drifted down the Nashwaak River in an inner tube to the tune of fifteen bucks while he nursed a beer. He made a few more stops before coming back to the motel. The odor of the carpet reminded him of the cinema. He tried to email Shastri with an update but couldn't find the words to describe their arrest, roller derbying Libyan virgins, and the fact that the lead they were now following was his boner for Bruce Dern. He gave up and decided to examine his medical kit. He pulled Tanuja's gun bag out of the closet and left it on the floor, then pulled out his kit from behind it. He pushed the laptop aside, and laid out his gear in an ordered manner on the small desk, and checked each article for quantity and cleanliness. This was a luxury he'd never enjoyed in the field. It gave him satisfaction. Then he packed it up and had a shower, where he again considered his lifelong sexual weirdness, and again became depressed, and again made up a song in his head about unicorns and the Olympics. "*Their horns were cheating the high jump! Bicycle seats, bicycle pump!*" It was brilliant, his best yet, but it didn't help. He was a creep and he knew it: he was the Raskolnikov of bicycle seat sniffers. He determined, as he did at least twice every day, to straighten the hell out.

He came out in a towel, and checked his phone. There was a message from his sister that said only "ANTS IN THE TRUCK."

He cocked a bemused eyebrow and set down the phone to get dressed, but there was a triple knock at the door in the exact rhythm of the opening drum riff of Slayer's "Raining Blood." "Room service!" the voice said.

"What?" Max said to himself. He clutched the knot in his towel and looked through the peephole. It was a woman with a food cart. "I didn't order any room service," Max said through the door. He didn't even know this place *had* room service now that he thought about it.

"Room service!" the woman said again. But there was something about the voice that penetrated him without his realizing it. It was as if once the woman had heard him speak, she had gained some fundamental understanding of his lesser mind and could use her own voice to press him in one direction or another.

Max huffed an exasperated sigh, and swung the door open to tell the woman off, but before he could say anything she shoved the cart at him, and he was forced to back up, nearly stumbling to let her in. She had perfect olive skin, and was wearing a ridiculous black and white maid's outfit that looked like it had come from a costume shop.

The cart was loaded with stainless steel mysteries, like little domed temples, and a hefty bottle of champagne on ice. She pushed the cart to the middle of the room, straightened herself up, and in the same insidious and commanding tone of voice as before, said, "Take off your towel."

So it *was* from a costume shop!

I must have heard an urban legend about this somewhere, Max thought. He scanned his memory trying to match any of the elements: cheap motel, room service, maid looking for sex. No, no correlations. This was something new. A sort of cultural milestone even, but, even as he thought this, he glanced over at the now empty 1.5 liter cup of Dr. Pepper he had bought for 36 cents at the Irving gas station on his way back to the motel and wondered if maybe he wasn't hallucinating the whole thing.

"Too slow," she said. And then, from somewhere in the cart, she produced a pistol. He recognized it: a Sprudla 44 from Slovakia. Very powerful and very illegal in this part of the world.

He whipped off the towel and threw it in the corner. He had an ass like a plank and a dick like yesterday's lettuce.

"You and your Mrs. need to get the fuck out of town. You can go back to Bangor and tell your boss Sue Wood that you snooped around like she asked but you turned up zilch."

Max remained frozen, staring at her with saucer-like, uncomprehending eyes. "She's not my Mrs.!" he managed to sputter.

"*Kull wahad!*" she barked. "Don't you get it?! Smith is starting to cotton on to you!"

"I don't – I don't know what you're talking about!"

Her lips compressed into a trembling, explosive line. She was edging towards eruption, but she could see the naked man standing in front of her was stubborn and an idiot, and knew only one thing would work. She pulled out her wallet and flipped it open at him.

"My name is Zilal al-Thani," she said. "RCMP. Listen to me. Pete Smith is involved in something bad. Very bad. And much bigger than any of this roller derby rivalry bullshit between him and your boss Sue Wood. I've been undercover in Pete Smith's team for the last two years and I don't need you and your mom fucking it up over some roller-skating garbage just when I'm about to crack this thing wide open. Now, start packing your fucking bags and –"

She picked up the duffel bag off the floor and dropped it on the bed. It was heavy as fuck and dropped with an industrial clank. "What the fuck?" she said.

"No, wait!" Max said, but he was too vulnerable to stop her.

The bag was packed to bursting point. When she unzipped it, it blossomed with gunmetal and ammunition. She shot a look at Max that was both accusatory and confused, like a spouse who's found a bag full of money hidden in the garage. She tucked her pistol into her lace-frilled apron and started rifling through the bag.

And then the door clicked open and a blast of cold night air rushed into the room. Tanuja was standing there with one hand on the knob and the other holding her key, her chartreuse and emerald sari resplendent in the revolting yellow light of the walkway.

"*Dey!*" she exclaimed in disgust. "Give him back his money. He doesn't need your business."

"Wait!" Max cried again, but it was too late.

The maid had spun and assumed a martial stance with her feet apart like a runner, and one fist above the other as if she were holding a steering wheel turned to a hard left. Tanuja had never seen it before and it unsettled her. But what made this more troubling was not only the unfamiliarity of it, but that Tanuja had recognized the woman's face from some of the photos of Gaddafi's entourage.

What Zilal saw was a woman in the doorway who looked about as easy to tip over as a fire hydrant.

Zilal turned her "steering wheel" hard to the right. The action hurtled her whole body off the ground, flipping up her ruffled maid skirt so you could see her garters, and twisting her into a weird, lightning-fast corkscrewing kick that propelled both feet into two blows that landed like cinder blocks against Tanuja's head. Tanuja reeled back and collided with the steel handrail in the walkway, but rebounded forward again. The stitches in her back had opened.

The maid was still in a recovery position with all her hands and feet on the ground, the feet crossed, and she was straightening up, like a ballet dancer in Swan Lake, with her back turned to Tanuja.

Tanuja ran up and kicked Zilal in the gut like she was a football.

"Nooj! Jesus Christ!" Max shrieked.

The kick flipped Zilal onto her back, but she grabbed Tanuja's leg, and flipped herself so the leg was locked, and Tanuja was pinned on her back with Zilal's fist pressed against her larynx. Only then did Max's exclamation register in Zilal's mind.

"What did you say?" she said.

"'Jesus Christ'…" he said. "The god of the white people."

"Before that!"

"…? 'Nooj?'"

Zilal's eyes widened. She looked down at the struggling woman beneath her, her sari, her smoky eyes, the red *pottu* on her forehead that seemed to pulse. She thought about the ferocity of the kick to stomach, like she'd been punched by a *Rajput* warrior, then looked up at the bag full of lethal steel on the bed, then back down at the woman.

"Holy shit," she breathed. "You're Tanuja Ramachandran."

***

Tanuja sat on the bed while Max re-stitched and bandaged her up. Zilal sat on the hard chair by the writing desk nursing a bitter sneer and a flask of whiskey to keep it taut. The sneer seemed to be a permanent feature only varying by degrees. Getting kicked in the gut by Tanuja had cranked it up to Billy Idol level.

Max finished up, closed up his bag and melted onto the sofa by the window so they were all facing each other. No one spoke for a minute while Tanuja inspected Zilal's ID. Finally satisfied, she tossed it across to her and broke the silence.

"Say that again," she said. "So you've been undercover for *three* years. One of those under Gaddafi…"

"Yeah."

"And two under Pete Smith."

"No. Under Banerji. After Gaddafi's regime crumbled, Banerji started picking up his now-former Revolutionary Nuns. The RCMP decided to leave me undercover to penetrate Banerji's operations. Three fucking years," she grumbled between slugs.

"Since when do Mounties work undercover

overseas?" Tanuja asked. It was more a statement than a question.

"Since 9/11. Ever since then, the RCMP has been CSIS's stooge. Whenever CSIS is short certain talents for an operation – say language or combat experience or being able to wipe one's own ass – they come around to the RCMP and pick and choose who they like. And there's nothing the RCMP can do about it except lick their balls and say thank you. That's how I ended up in Tripoli."

"You're telling me the Canadian Secret Intelligence Service needs to recruit black ops agents externally?"

"They don't call it Canadian for nothing."

"So how did Pete Smith come into this?" Max interjected.

"He didn't," Zilal said. "Banerji came to him. Or I should say, Banerji came to Fredericton with all the Virgins, me included, and we haven't seen him since. He told us Smith would approach us to join his... roller derby team... and we should do as he asked. But not all Nuns are created equal. Some of the higher-ranked, more trusted ones still keep in regular touch with Banerji. They're up to something. Something big. I'm still trying to figure out what that is. Once I do, I'm out."

Tanuja said: "So Banerji ordered Smith to recruit the women?"

"I don't know that he did. I think Pete just likes roller derby and... a certain type of woman. Enough that Banerji knew what would happen if Pete's old team got offers that were too tempting elsewhere, and then we were basically offered to him on a plate."

She had called him "Pete." After three years, Tanuja wondered if the real Zilal still existed anymore, and where her loyalties really lay. Even if she got out, what would she do with herself? What *could* she?

"But why?"

"Banerji is using Pete's money to enhance the Nuns for a bigger operation."

Tanuja's jaw line squirmed like her glands were juicing venom. "Srikanth Balu." The name dripped from her.

"You know him?!"

"I know him…" Tanuja seemed to be speaking to someone else, from somewhere else, far away.

Her mind was coalescing into that singular focus it sometimes took before it detonated and turned everyone around her into red blotches. Max could see it in her face, but he pressed on. "What about Balu and these enhancements?" he asked.

"Balu's the one that introduced us to Smith. The enhancements are ostensibly to make us better roller derby players, or at least that's what it sounds like whenever Smith talks about it. But, see, I don't know. I'm in the control group. I wasn't going to volunteer for that shit. It's mostly the women who compete get the treatments anyway. There's a lab under the house but only a few of them are ever allowed down there, women who were with Gaddafi a lot longer than I was. Anyway, whatever it is, it's not steroids. Smith would never break the rules. You can get a whiff of it sometimes though. Stinks like fuck. Smith owns that Smell-o-whatever downtown too. People act weird around that place. My money says it's a front for whatever Balu's working on. A testing chamber, you might say."

Max was about to ask her what she meant by "compete," but Tanuja cut him off. "I need to get down there," Tanuja said. She looked at Zilal but her eyes were going right through her, to another place.

Zilal sniffed and snapped the empty flask into her garter. "Never gonna happen. You know, I saw your file once at RCMP HQ in Ottawa," she said as she pulled a bottle of Schooner out of the mini bar. She snapped the top off on the edge of the desk, skulled it down to the base of the neck, then sat down again. "Thought they'd pulled the dossier on Countess Bathory by mistake. But not even you could get in there. The house guards all came in through Banerji's pipeline too."

"Fourteen women," Tanuja shrugged. "Plus some wet-behind-the-ears guards. Cannon fodder."

"Fourteen? Heh. Ha. He's got fourteen women *on the track*. There are twenty-six women in that house – Revolutionary Nuns, plus some of Banerji's own, and the hired gun security guys."

Wide-eyed silence.

"Gaddafi never stopped collecting those 'virgins,'" she snorted. "And he got them from everywhere – all over the Middle East and Africa and even as far away as Vietnam and India and Venezuela. Hell, at the end there he was even trying to recruit Condoleezza Rice."

"Condy's a virgin?!" lamented Max.

"I don't know about that. But I do know that man loved to eat pussy and something about her turned him horny as a triceratops blaring La Cucaracha. Fucked up his neck so bad from it, he had to get surgery on his C7 vertebra."

"Jesus Christ," Max exclaimed.

"God of the white people, right?" Zilal saluted Max with her Schooner and clicked her tongue. "Anyway, Pete thinks maybe you're working for Sue Wood. And Flora suspects worse. You'll need to watch your back."

Tanuja lay back on the bed and looked at the ceiling, trying to digest and process it all. "The delivery truck was full of cases of ants," she said, and then was silent as she drifted into sleep. She had a dream about Divali firecrackers spinning on the ground and spraying purple sparks in the night, and Poppins candies bought from a street stall in Madras, their rainbow colors sticking to her fingers, glistening and invincible against the noise and the dirt.

***

An hour later, Tanuja was still asleep. Zilal used the opportunity to demand Max give her some of his clothes. She wore his suits better than he did.

Meanwhile, on the motel room TV, Greg Flynn, the city sheriff was on the nine o'clock news holding a press conference advising the men of Fredericton, for their own wellbeing, to stop jerking off in public. The headline at the bottom of the screen read: "JERK OFF EPIDEMIC." Apparently, more than one person had been seriously injured jerking off beyond the safety of their own homes. One astute reporter asked if the unspecified number of incidents might have happened in the vicinity of the Smell-O-Vision cinema, even though the sheriff had never mentioned – what Max knew – that one of the "victims" was the theater's projectionist. The reporter was connecting the wrong dots and getting the same picture. The sheriff talked his way around it, but Max could see in his expression a kind of suppressed doubt, that Flynn himself wanted to draw that same connection but was making every effort to keep his own mouth shut. He was a man who had lost control over his own town. People were jerking off like crazy, or worse, and there was nothing he could do about it except issue advisories. He was in somebody's pocket. The news moved on to something about the Prime Minister.

"I knew one of those guys," Zilal said between slugs of her third Schooner. She carried it around by the neck, as though she were a three-year old with her hand around the throat of the pet cat. "She *did* do it, didn't she," she said to him. It wasn't a question.

Max answered by turning off the TV and tossing the remote to the opposite corner of the sofa. He walked out onto the walkway to get away from her but she followed him out. In the autumn darkness the silhouettes of the maple leaves on the trees behind the forsaken service garage across the road were like thousands of Gremlin claws clutching at the sky. She lit a cigarette while he rested his elbows on the rail and watched the black river lap a languid, pressing rhythm.

"Is it true about what happened to her family?" she said to him.

"You read her file," he answered without looking at her. "They were my family too. I hardly saw them, but they were great kids." He recalled the picture of them she carried in her purse.

Zilal took a drag. "So who sent you?"

"What do you mean? Why do you think someone sent us?"

"TR doesn't strike me as the kind of woman that cares so much about details, but she was asking a lot of questions in there."

"Wasn't that in her file too?" he sniggered.

She was still waiting for her answer.

Of course she doesn't know, he thought. *She works for CSIS. They don't know anything.* "Indian embassy," he said.

"Why the fuck is she working for *anybody*?"

"For her, they're resources she can turn on almost like a tap. Money, weapons," he answered without looking at her. "To them… she's a guided missile."

"And you? You don't seem like you belong here."

"I'm her field medic."

"I can see that, but come on."

He didn't answer until she stood on his foot. "You could say I'm the guidance system."

"And she stands for that?"

"I'm her brother."

"Okay. So?"

"Could you please get off my foot?" he grimaced. She did.

"I'm not really sure why she stands for it," he said, trailing off.

"But?"

He looked out over the black lapping river and remembered the look in Tanuja's eyes, the desolation, as they stared at that glorious Dali in the art gallery. "What if," he said already foreseeing the hollowness of his own words. "What if she's not too far gone?" he ventured.

"What do you mean?" Zilal asked with suspicion.

"I can save her," he answered in a heated whisper. "Maybe. I think she wants to be saved. Maybe she wants to come back, to be in *this* world again. To finally feel something besides hate and sadness again. You're incredulous. But you know what's not in her file? She sends all her money to orphanages in India."

"So what? What are you? Her psychiatrist?"

"No, but I'm *seeing* a psychiatrist. I think I can do

it. Maybe she thinks so too. I owe her everything. She protected me after our parents died and in the orphanage. She tried to make life seem a bit normal. And she rescued me from that place. And I'm all the family she's got left. I'm the last thread, the bread crumbs that can lead her back."

Zilal had been listening to all this dumbstruck. Now, she huffed and said, "She's a slave."

That snapped him out of his melancholy reverie.

"What do you mean?" he asked.

"She must've taken care of everyone involved in that horror with her family by now. So now her revenge-seeking is more like a franchise. It's expanded. More targets. I've seen it a dozen times. That unspeakable thing, it's like it rewrote her brain. She's computerized now. Kill, kill, kill. You said it yourself. She's a guided missile, there to be exploited by anyone that can manipulate her malfunctioning programming. You'll never 'save' her. She's not even capable of *wanting* to be free. Hell, you just said you're her field medic. If anything you're her goddamn enabler! *That's* why she stands for it! And as long as she's working for the embassy, they'll want her short-circuiting brain to just keep on that way. She's a slave to her own mind and a slave to the embassy."

Max had to admit to himself the truth of her words. Even *he* had always known it and he was just a flunky. Max had tried to convince himself that Nooj aligning with the embassy was something that linked her back to "normal society," the first step or the backdrop to her full recovery. But the embassy was *not* normal society. It was as toxic as any of the other agencies, maybe even worse because their wetworks operations were carried out under the table and they were unaccountable. Now that he thought about it, it was almost like Tanuja and the embassy were psychically linked. Those ties would have to be severed. That was something he'd known all along too, though he hadn't wanted to admit it.

He didn't dare reveal to Zilal that he sometimes caught Tanuja mumbling to herself, and it seemed to him, gathered from various clues over the years, that she was talking to Lakshmibai, the Rani of Jhansi.

He also didn't dare reveal that his reasons were selfish too, that maybe by saving Tanuja he could redeem himself too.

The door opened behind them, and Tanuja came out wearing a black sari trimmed with cerulean bands and falling peacock feathers in gold and Casper The Friendly Ghost white. "How long has that K-car been parked over there?" Her voice was like the crunch of tires on gravel.

Zilal and Max turned at once and looked at the dilapidated lot across the road. There was indeed a 1988 Plymouth Reliant parked there behind the fence, facing the motel, where one hadn't been before. Max looked back at Tanuja with remorseful eyes.

"*Badava* rascal!" she cursed at him.

She drew an ornate *kattari* push dagger out from

her purse. The blade was a ten-inch long isosceles triangle shape, a few inches across at the base and attached to a handle that recalled ladder rungs at 90 degrees. You gripped it with a fist and punched rather than slashed with it. Simultaneously, Zilal pulled her pistol from under the side of her that was covered.

"That's Safeera's car over there," Zilal said. "One of the skaters. If she's seen me over here I'm fucked."

Max started to head back into the motel room, but Tanuja grabbed his arm. "What are you doing?" she asked.

"I'm going to prep my medical kit," he said. "Again."

The two women descended the metal stairs to the ground level together like smoke and slinked past the parked cars. When they got across the road, the light from the streetlamps was decent enough to make out shoeprints in the sand and…

Tanuja froze.

From two steps ahead, Zilal had heard Nooj stop and whispered, "What is it?" There was still no answer. She backtracked and looked down at the ground, following Tanuja's wide-eyed line of sight.

Animal tracks. Large paw prints.

"What…?"

Tanuja unfroze, her gaze darting all over the grounds, her breath short. Her neck was already wet and glistening under the street light.

"It prefers… it prefers dark places," she managed. *I*

will not fear, she began to recite to herself in her mind.

"Hey, what the hell's the matter with…"

Safeera flew out of the bushes from behind them screaming, "Traitor!" and clotheslined Zilal against the hood of the Reliant, her every movement accompanied by the slink of a chain. Zilal bounced off the hood and crumpled to the ground like a discarded puppet. Tanuja's immediate instinct was to shiv Safeera with the *kattari*, but the sound of the chain transfixed her. It was attached to the Virgin's left wrist and ended at a leash around the neck of the Monkey Man of New Delhi.

11

It was the fourth night: May 13, 2001. It would be the final night, Tanuja was determined of that. Or at least, that's what she had told herself, but as she charged through the labyrinthine bazaar pursuing the thing, teeth gritted, *pottu* smeared with glistening sweat across her forehead, the embarrassing hubris of any such claim was only too obvious to her.

The canvas tops of the stalls crowded around her, the dark was polluted by the dirty light of oil lamps hung here and there. It stunk of piss and feces and frying oil and piles and piles of fish, heaped on top of each other like garbage, their eyes staring up at her aghast, hopeless, desperate. Filth sloshed through the dim gutters, spectral shit in the oily lights. The ground was dusty, but there were no tracks. She followed the pleading, wailing, shouting cries. Anger, fear, pain. The thing had ripped through here, fast. She had seen it move, and she could picture it now, down on all fours like a cheetah. Tanuja saw a woman in her sixties who looked a hundred, her arm slashed open, blood pouring out, tears streaming down the infinite creases of her face. "How could such a thing happen?" she was crying in Hindi. The people nearby saw Tanuja, brandishing her Berakna AR-15, and crowded around her, their savior. A woman with a slashed face – four clean "claw" marks – grabbed Tanuja's sari like a beggar, words spilling out of her but meaning nothing. "Hanuman," she said, over and over again. "Hanuman, Hanuman." *The monkey god*. A drop of sweat fell from Tanuja's chin, landed on the woman's face, and trickled past one of her wounds. A man whose fruit cart had been knocked over yelled at her, as if she had done it. Well, she had a gun so she was responsible as far as he cared.

Three nights this had been going on. Three nights the thing had evaded her, but tonight she was close — so close the wailing women and screaming stall holders were right there in her face. At this level nobody knew what it really was, not even Tanuja, but it had to be a man, didn't it? One man wearing steel claws. And here she was packing more heat than a Kenner Easy-Bake Oven. The higher-ups had sent her out here. "Clean it up," they said. Their exact words. Maybe they knew something. The vibe felt bad, but Tanuja was the gun, not the gunman. She fired in the direction she was pointed.

"Which way?" she asked in a thick accent to anyone

who would answer. They all gestured in a general direction up the street, like a fleshy arrow, a wave that surged forward with her. A hunched, wrinkled crone, so dark her head and arms were almost invisible in the darkness, grabbed Tanuja's arm and led her to the open entry arch of a tenement block about fifty meters further up the dusty, crowded street. The arch was a black maw, with dirty steps going up just inside. The throng washed back leaving her alone at the vanguard – this was a shore they wouldn't touch.

Tanuja's nerves were on fire, and her stomach had tied itself into a Calabi-Yau manifold. There was a TV commercial in constant rotation at the time for Poppins, the poor man's Lifesavers, sung to the tune of Madonna's "Like a Virgin." She sung it to herself in the hopes it would calm her. It didn't.

Lick a Poppins!
You could even lick seven or nine!

Tanuja went in, her black sari melting into the darkness, and started up the leaf and sand-strewn stairs. There were fresh cries further up, more casualties, frightened children, woken babies. She followed the sounds, the claw marks on the walls, the burgundy streaks, looked in the apartment doors that were open, and found one on the top floor that looked as if the thing had swept through it like a shrapnel-loaded twister. She bolted through, following its wake. No one in the home had any fear left for the hard AR-15 that came with her. She went to a shattered window, smashed out the rest of the glass and frame, had a brief nap leaning against the wall, then climbed onto the window frame, and leapt to the roof opposite, just like the thing must have because she had seen the impact crater it left in the dust over there.

She rolled, righted herself into a half crouch, her sari scuffed but not ripped. But the rooftop was infested – like the rest of Delhi – with rhesus macaque monkeys, silhouetted against the dim wash of light and tireless cries from the street. She stood and raised her rifle to shoulder height, stalking forward. The macaques were annoyed by her presence, their protests were guttural and aggressive. It had to be a man, right? She remembered her *kalaripayattu* training: *vigneswa* – strength, *channiga* – patience.

A ball of shit hit her in the back. She pivoted, deflecting a second one with her rifle. But it left her open and something big – larger than a macaque, smaller than a man – leapt and knocked her to the ground, blasting three shots from the AR-15 into the air, and sprang away again. She was getting up when one of the rhesus monkeys – thrown – smashed into her hip. Then another hit her, then another in the head this time, and another, but she swatted the last one out of the way, and no more came. The macaques were shrieking in the dark, and finally she spotted the creature, just the outline of the thing, at the edge of the roof, and it was running towards her, accelerating, while she was still trying to regain her bearings after a fucking monkey had been lobbed at her head. She saw the shiny green dome of its helmet coming towards her at ramming speed, and then it was too late because the helmet slammed right into her gut and she was airborne, and then had the wind knocked out of her again as she hit the floor. So much for *vadugashcha* – the posture.

She got up on one knee like a drunk and started to raise the gun but it was kicked away. Long gone now, she could hear it skidding across the ground, too far away. Her attacker slashed at her and she rolled with it just in time, but it carved open her left shoulder through her sari, her sari of the finest silk, now with three gaping, wet wounds. The thing never lost its balance, but Tanuja did manage to duck and start to run from it. Run because it was not a man. It was a creature: four feet tall, covered in fur, with four-inch steel claws, a metal helmet, and a T-shirt with a faded *Last Starfighter* iron on print. A fear overcame her as she realized it was not an earthly thing. It coursed through her whole body, just under her skin. Its joints were so strange, almost backwards. Was it a *vetala* – a spirit in a corpse? Its red marble eyes were soulless, like it was a thing from out of time, like something she'd seen before and forgotten, a black thing that watched her in the night as a child as she slept in her bed and was still standing there looking back at her when she opened her eyes.

As she sprinted away from it, fighting through the

fear and pain, the image flashed into Tanuja's mind of a similar shirt that she saw the Minister of the Interior's son wearing at his house the other day.

But there was no time for that now. Still the Madonna jingle for Poppins cycled through her thoughts:

Suck a Poppins!

They are not a mountain to climb!

She stumbled, found a can of food the monkeys had stolen and flung it back at him: useless. Stumbled again, and found a plank, whipped it around just in time as the Monkey Man had vaulted at her from ten feet back and she managed to catch him in midair. He almost landed on his feet but slipped on a banana peel and went face first into a pile of shit. The macaques were loving the show and applauded and shrieked with delight. The baby ones were little balls of cuteness. Tanuja found the door down into the building, went through, slammed it behind her, and started bolting down the stairs, while reaching for the tiny Lohals .38 tucked into her sari petticoat at the small of her back. The door burst open, she turned and blasted the creature in the shoulder. An infuriated roar spewed out of its throat. Tanuja went down a flight, walked into someone's apartment, where a shocked family started to exclaim, but she put her finger to her lips and held up her gun so it was visible. The family huddled together in a corner.

Every motion of her torso came with agony so searing she was amazed her entire left side was still attached at all. Her sari was soaked with blood and sweat and getting heavier every second. And the world was becoming dimmer, but she was not falling asleep. She knew that. That shivering family in the corner was fading to black. She did not want to die here. No, no, no. In her weakening consciousness she could hear approaching steps. The *vetala* was coming to kill her, kill her like she was a child, and she was so afraid. No, no, no. To go into the blackness of non-life in this terror. She fell to her knees, her gun pointed at the door, and the tears came and came. And when the door splintered apart and the furry thing came through with its gurgling scream, she blasted it in the torso, the act of pulling the trigger torturing her wounds, and fur went out the exit wound and the thing fell back with the silence and finality of death. Tanuja fell down too, to die, and she thought of her husband and her children, while she heard the screams of the living around her.

Eat a Po-o-op-pins!
Try the lemon and then the li-i-i-ime!

***

Zilal started to haul herself up off the ground, groaning and balancing against the Reliant to support her aching back. She'd lost her gun. She saw Tanuja, standing there frozen and wide-eyed, the *kattari* still in white-knuckle grip in her hand. Why wasn't she doing anything? Some meters away was Safeera, pulling a long, curved Persian *shamshir* sword from its sheath with a slow, slick metal sound. When it was free she took a step towards them, teeth gritted. But then there was the clink of chain, and a four-foot tall manimal lumbered in front of her with heavy breaths, reached a hand up to her chest to stop her. It continued to limp forwards towards Tanuja.

It stopped and looked at her, baring its uneven yellow teeth, its chest rising and falling. Even Zilal was transfixed. And then it spoke. Spoke with the labored, straining voice of a beast raised in the jungle by Marlon Brando. "Me..." it said tapping its chest with a manacled paw, "Last Starfighter." And just below where it tapped was a large bullet hole you could see clear through, and seeing it only made everything worse for Tanuja as the black, swirling, hard marble of rage in her solar plexus that automated her became clouded over by immobilizing terror. Malfunction, system shutdown. The thing she thought dead was here, alive, the *original*. It could have been her moment of revenge. The scar across her chest was even pulsing, but her id was like a beaten dog before it.

The Monkey Man sprang at Tanuja, in that same arc it had leapt at her twelve years ago. But in the same instant a 1990 Ford Taurus slammed into the creature and sent it flying with an animal yelp into some dark brambles at the rear of the lot, tugging Safeera down into the dirt when the chain pulled taut. The car screeched to a stop, spitting up dirt.

The driver was Oilers Toque Man.

"Bobcats," he said across through the passenger side window to her. "Around these parts, very bad news."

Tanuja came to her senses and circled around to the driver side door, yanking it open. "Shove over," she commanded.

"Madam… are you sure you know how to handle this vehicle?" he said as he shuffled across the seats. He turned at the sound of Zilal slamming the back door shut.

Nooj gave an Indian head bobble and slammed the Taurus into gear. The engine block roared like a jungle cat, rumbled up through her feet and legs, through her pussy, up past that black marble in her torso, through her spine, and ignited her hippocampus. She threw it into reverse and the car started to scream backwards.

Just then the Monkey Man bounded out of the brambles and dug his four-inch steel claws into the roof of the Taurus, wrenching it off, but losing his balance so he and the roof hit the ground with a monstrous clang. Zilal took advantage of the makeshift convertible roof, and managed to fire three shots before Tanuja floored the gas and shot them off up the road, through an empty stretch in the direction of the airport.

"Goodness me!" said Oilers Toque Man. "My car!"

"Is this your car?" said Tanuja.

"No, madam. No. I stole it."

"Where's your friend, Bolo?"

"Gone," Oilers Toque Man said. "Like all the others."

"Here they come!" shouted Zilal as the Reliant's predatory headlights began to grow larger through the rear window. She raised herself up and started firing again. "They're going to try to sideswipe us!" she shouted over the gunfire.

"I like your friend," Oilers Toque Man said.

"She's not my friend. She's RCMP."

Bolo was "gone" he'd said, but he didn't need to elaborate. With every bullet Zilal fired, a piece fell into place for Tanuja with deafening finality. All the missing over the past year – test subjects for whatever Banerji was doing to them. Mostly homeless. It was perfect. The city had the highest number of millionaires per capita of any city in Canada. As long as none of their own were among the lost, there was no reason for the police to feel any pressure to follow-up the cases, and the rich assholes would even be quietly happy to see fewer people like Bolo around. But did Pete Smith know about it?

The Reliant sideswiped the Taurus sending it into a 135 degree skid.

"What the fuck's the matter with you?!" Zilal shouted. "I told you they were going to do that!"

The Reliant had come to a stop and was now reversing towards them from fifty meters up ahead. Big mistake. Nooj spun the Taurus around and rammed them full speed in the rear bumper. Safeera and the Monkey Man crashed through the front windshield, bounced off the hood, and splashed onto the pavement. Oilers Toque Man and Zilal were unconscious, but Tanuja poured out of the Taurus like it was a clown car, sari flapping and *kattari* drawn. When she came around to the front of the Reliant, shattered glass across the pavement, Safeera was there, dead, the chain still attached to her wrist, but at the other end, the manacle was broken and empty. The headlights of the Reliant highlighted a trail of black blood drifting off the road and into the woods.

No. Safeera was alive. She stumbled up, finding her feet and nursing her head. There were pieces of glass in her face and hands. Then she sensed the emptiness of the chain and deflated, forgetting the pain in her head when she saw the broken manacle. She turned and saw the ornate, triangular blade trained on her, and the veiny, white-knuckled fist that gripped it, and drew her *shamshir*.

She wheezed through her crushed glass visage and limped to the side, as if to pace around Tanuja, the chain dragging across the concrete. After the sound of the crash, Tanuja was now wishing she'd simply armed herself with a Moshult 9 mm anyway, when from behind her, Zilal shot Safeera in the chest, sending her flat onto the pavement with a tinkle and crunch of windshield beneath her. Tanuja and Zilal looked at each other. Tanuja said, "We could have gotten information out of her," and Zilal said, "She recognized me, and she might have gotten away," and they understood each other, though neither had spoken out loud. Tanuja stomped on Safeera's DG sunglasses and crushed them underfoot.

After a moment Safeera started to get up again. Zilal shot her in the head this time, turning her into a lifeless glass-studded mass in the road, illuminated by the headlights of the K-Car, vapor and dust seemingly rising up from her body.

Headlights came up the road and came to a stop behind them, and they turned to look. It was Max. He got out and approached them with his medical kit, looked at the two cars, the body, the broken manacle, then opened his kit up on the hood of the Reliant, and found a bandage to put on Zilal's forehead.

12

At 10 p.m., General Will Stump was still awake and watching dash cam crash videos on YouTube when the banging at the door blasted across the house. What a nuisance! The worst kind of intrusion. Everyone at Base Gagetown knew not to disturb the general in his "quarters" (actually a two-story Dutch Colonial Revival built in 1920, and maintained in good condition for generations of generals) after dark. He quickly lumbered out of his chair in his nightgown and slippers, and shuffled out of the office with a phlegmy grumble, pausing for a second at the stairs to listen and make sure his significant other or daughter hadn't woken at the sound. The banging came again, and the general shushed at it irefully, as if anyone on the other side of the door could hear him. His slippers slapped on the hardwood as he crossed the floor, and when he wrenched the door open with a "What the goddamn f—," he stopped short and his gummy white face fell.

The man on the other side on the porch was a tall Indian, maybe 6'5", in a long dark coat. He had falcon-like features and exuded stillness even as he turned from enjoying the dark view of the grounds to look at Stump.

"It's cold out here on a fall night," the man said amiably.

"Banerji," Stump said. The word was said like an invocation, but Stump's eyes were trying to exorcise him.

"It's so cold, I think you should invite me in, Will."

Stump stepped through the door and closed it behind him. "What are you doing here? What do you want?" He put his hand on Banerji's shoulder and led him further away from the door, down the porch steps.

"I want my merchandise," Banerji said when they were on the grass.

"What?! Now?!" Spittle flew from Stump's lips even though he whispered.

A light flicked on in an upstairs window. Stump pushed Banerji further along and out of the window's line of sight, to the front of the three-car garage.

"This wasn't the deal!" Stump blubbered. "I don't have to deliver for three more weeks, and we were never supposed to meet face to face!"

General Stump was no small man and had been involved in many overseas conflicts, all embarked on to best please and kowtow to Canada's American overlords, but even so he felt like Banerji was a vampiric void in the darkness of the driveway, lit only by dim, far off streetlights, and the Keralan's gravity was going to absorb and crush him. Banerji didn't reply to Stump's consternation. He simply looked at Stump like he'd look at a Niagara Falls snow globe. At last he said, with an unexpectedly duckish smile in his hawkish face, "You surprise me, Will. Acting like anything you say matters when –"

"Don't say it," Stump grumbled, shaking his head.

"I've got recordings of all those phone calls you made in Afghanistan! And here you are acting like I can't visit you at all hours and get you to take me to see my merchandise in your house robe! You've got real guts, Will. I like you, even if –"

"Don't say it, you goddamn vulture."

"– you're the kind of guy who firebombs orphans and then talks about it on the phone. Now go get your keys to your Hummer, son, and let's go see all my shiny new gear."

Stump's slippers flapped against the concrete all the way back to the door. When he came back with the keys, Banerji was looking around the neighborhood again as though he were in a Bob Ross painting.

"It's cold out here on a fall night," he said again.

They got into the Hummer and started driving across the base, Stump's sweaty pout never left his face from the moment he put the key in the ignition.

"How old are you, Will?"

"Sixty-two," he answered through gritted teeth. *Is he going to say it?* Banerji thought. "Too old for this shit," he continued.

Banerji clapped and laughed like there'd been an explosion at the nitrous oxide factory. Stump didn't respond, didn't even know what Banerji found so funny. He kept his eyes on the road with a snarl and tried to work the Hummer's pedals with slippers on his feet.

"You have a big house, Will. You have a significant other? Kids?"

"Married twenty-three years, this time," he answered through a curled lip, though the house had nothing to do with the size of his family. "Daughter's twenty-one. She'll be moving out soon enough. Got a son from a long time back too. Don't see him a lot."

"You know, Will, I know what you you're thinking. You're thinking, 'So what if that shit in Afghanistan gets out?' You're only three years away from retirement anyway. Kids are grown up, your reputation won't affect them. Would the Canadian people care about a bunch of dead brown kids anyway, so far away and ten years ago? Is this it up here?" he said pointing at a large hangar out the window.

"No," Stump said, "we gotta drive the whole way across the base."

"Well, the answer, is No, Will. No one will care, and it will flare like a match for thirty seconds and people will scroll past it on their Facebook feeds. And the government will *say* they disciplined you, but, really, they'll give you a nice retirement package, won't they, Will? You could just let the truth out. And you know it. So why are you driving me to see my toys at ten at night in your Hummer in your bathrobe? What were you doing anyway? Watching dash cam videos?"

Stump looked at him in surprise.

Banerji laughed again, a sound with all the mirth of a body being dragged from a river. "I really do like you, Will. You're a complex guy. Not like some people. Like this woman I know, her brain only works one way. Like a toy train track that's just a single circle going around and around with no hills or tunnels or post offices. If you wrote a book about her, it would only be one sentence long. Sometimes she drives me so crazy I just want to rip her fucking head off!!" He started jabbing the air with an imaginary knife. He had to calm himself, slow down, make himself take deep breaths. He pulled a handkerchief out of his jacket and dabbed his forehead. "Anyway, Will, the question was, why are you still here? Do you know what I'm going to do with my merchandise?"

Stump shook his head at the road, sighing.

"Now, you're being insincere, Will. I think you have a pretty good idea what I'm going to do. I mean, with gear like that, what else could I be planning? And I think we're still here having this conversation precisely *because* you know. We're here *because* your bosses would give you a gold watch even after you killed those kids because they're perfectly happy to have those kids dead. And you hate your own government for being that way. But you'll always remember those kids, Will. Sometimes a good man does bad things. And sometimes it takes a bad man to do a good thing. And I think deep inside you believe I'm going to do a good thing. This country did some very bad things to me. They deserve comeuppance. I'm like those kids, Will. I'm those kids!"

Stump gritted his teeth in anger at Banerji's flippant goading. "I got no idea what the fuck you *think* you're doing, but this is a *bad* time to be getting up to any sort of shit in this town! Do you have any idea? Goddamn bobcat attacks, missing people, some sorta jerk off epidemic was on the news tonight, and believe me there's some fishy business with that Smith theater downtown, and all those damned Amazons of his – something fishy about them too –" He stopped mid-thought.

Banerji was smiling at him, and almost felt sorry for him. Stump would never be privy to the big picture in the background, but Banerji could see that Stump had started to suspect that it was all connected and Banerji was responsible for all of it. Stump emitted the sigh of a miserable man driving a Hummer in his bathrobe at night.

They came to a stop in front of a row of hangars, each even bigger than the one they'd passed earlier.

They clambered out, and Stump led the way to Number 6 with plodding full-body Muppet steps. He stopped in front of the security panel and looked at the keys in his hand, then at Banerji, dry yet slimy, almost like Stump expected to see flecks of dried blood around his lips. Banerji was looking back at Stump with a dead still, million-volt laser beam gaze. It took Stump a second to collect himself but then he inserted the key into the panel, punched in the security code, and stood back as the giant hangar doors started to slide open from the middle with a heavy metallic scraping. They stopped with a clang.

Stump had a flashlight on his keychain that he used to find the panel of light switches inside. He threw them all on and flooded the hangar with light. For a moment, Banerji wondered if somewhere on the drive between Stump's residence and the hangar, he had stopped caring if anyone found out he was out here. A man in despair could be a dangerous piece to have on the game board, but in fact he was more blusterous than ever, and the hardware arranged around the hangar was so glimmering and fantastical that Banerji could have happily just shot him anyway and been done with it regardless of the consequences. "This is the kind of shiny goodness," he said, "that even a thousand *crore* rupees couldn't buy."

Banerji came to a gleaming weapons rack right at the front, but it was not weapons that it was arrayed with. "I'm going to try on a pair." Banerji said, sitting on a nearby stool. "Size 12."

Stump gave him permission with a dismissive wave and a tight-lipped scowl, then disappeared to get at some more light switches.

A patrol jeep screeched up outside the hangar, and the white soldier driving leapt out with his firearm drawn and pointed at Banerji. "Hands up, towel head! Identify yourself! Identify yourself! Down on your stomach with your hands behind your head! Identify yourself! I said down on your stomach or I will fire!" The soldier bee-lined into the bright lights of the hangar. Banerji's hands were up, but he was still seated and he wasn't about to lie down on the cold concrete. The soldier was reaching for his radio when Stump reemerged.

"Oh, oh, p-pardon me, sir! I didn't realize it was you," the soldier spluttered, his words even more mangled in taking in the general's attire. His eyes flashed back over to Banerji, and Stump caught the glance.

"Holster the weapon, son," the general said. "Showing an old friend around the base."

"O-of course, sir. Well, I have to say, haha, if you're going to see some sights, you're never going to beat Hangar 6. I-it's like Buck Rogers or something in here. I'll, uh, I'll just radio this in. Standard procedure."

Banerji flexed his big toe, and a spray of bullets exploded out of the size 12 roller skates he had just laced up. The soldier splashed onto the floor like a month-old lasagna.

"Gun cleaning accident," Banerji said to a jaw-quivering Stump. "I'm expecting many more such accidents to follow. I'd like the thirteen other pairs too, please."

***

Tanuja and Zilal decided to feed Safeera to the beavers.

The Monkey Man had escaped into the woods leaving behind a trail of blood on the concrete and no more. After ten, fifteen, twenty muscle-numbing minutes of waiting in stillness for a surprise attack, they risked venturing back into action, and had to make some decisions.

They could leave everything as it was, torch the cars, and make it look like Safeera died in a car wreck. But if the bones survived the blaze so would the bullet hole in her head. Also, if Safeera was found dead at all, on the day of Aaliyah's funeral no less, it would only raise more alarms and further hinder Tanuja from reaching her objective. Tanuja also suggested that they get rid of the body and Oilers Toque Man wait at the scene, and if and when any officials showed up, he should confess to jerking off while driving and causing the accident, from which the driver of the other car walked away. This story had too many holes in it for the others. They could have pushed the smashed cars into the river, but they'd only float up. In the end, they decided to take the license plates off the smashed cars and push them onto the bank of a tributary of the river in plain sight where they already found a colony of refrigerators, mattresses, and shopping carts. Safeera's body went into the trunk of Tanuja's car along with Max's surgical knives and the *shamshir*, and she drove further up along the river with Zilal in the passenger seat and Max and Oilers Toque Man in the back, up to where the beavers lived.

When they got to a decent spot, she parked in a clear area of river bank and got to work on the body with Zilal. Max kept his distance, and kept watch with Oilers Toque Man. When Oilers Toque Man caught sight of what they were doing, he cringed and said to Max, "From what I've seen so far, I imagine your sister is often involved in this sort of… Grand Guignol." Max only frowned at him (they were using his scalpels to do the job), then looked up the term on his phone with his back turned to him.

Once the women had diced Safeera into small enough pieces, they threw them close to the water's edge and within minutes a pair of beavers came waddling out of the river to feast. They threw out more meat, this time out into the water where it plopped in, leaving dark ripples. More beavers came splashing along. There seemed to be another one every thirty seconds.

Tanuja did the deed in grim silence, but Zilal had the faintest curve of satisfaction on her lips, barely discernible in the moonlight. "God, I hated this woman," she said, and she lobbed in a whole thigh. It kersplashed into the river and the beavers swarmed it like cartoon piranhas. "The shit I saw her do to people in Libya…" Zilal's voice trailed off, and Tanuja knew she must have had to do the same undercover right alongside her. She didn't seem to have any problem cutting a woman up under cover of darkness and feeding her parts to the local semiaquatic rodents. "Good riddance," she muttered, and drop kicked a whole hand.

She got a cigarette out of her purse and lit it. "So," she said. "Are you gonna tell me what the fuck that thing was back there, or what?"

"In May of 2001," Tanuja began, "reports started to circulate around New Delhi about a four-foot-tall monkey-like person with –"

"You don't need to describe it."

"None of the descriptions were quite the same. He would appear at night and leap from rooftop to rooftop and attack people, slashing them with his steel claws. Sometimes he even threw them down stairwells or right off the buildings. It only took one night, that first night of attacks, for mass hysteria and pandemonium to break out. And each night after the first there were more attacks and it was like the panic was igniting the whole city. Finally, after a few more days of this, I got called in by the Ministry of the Interior. They said it was a Pakistani special forces soldier who'd snapped and they needed him eighty-sixed to avoid a war."

"The Ministry of the Interior?"

Tanuja nodded with equal incredulity. "Of course. Because when I tracked the thing down the next night, it was no soldier, and it was wearing a shirt I'd seen the Minister's son wearing earlier. I can put two and two together. It was no Pakistani. It was something *we* had unleashed, and had enough free rein to go into the Minister's house and raid his son's closet."

"But you couldn't put a bullet through its head."

"I put a hole in its heart. Although, apparently that doesn't count for anything. It left me for dead too. Heart stopped for three minutes. Shredded my shoulder and my tit, haven't been able to move it right since." The scar tingled when she said it. "The man who made it was Balu, and a few nights back I turned some very hirsute and agile bastards into sieves in Montreal. Thugs in Banerji's employ."

Zilal processed it all for a few seconds, watching the silhouettes of the beavers surface and dive in the oil-black river. "Some of the team are stronger than they were during the Gaddafi days," she said, "but it's not like Balu's down there gene splicing them to monkeys."

"The Monkey Man is hard to kill, but he's crude. Banerji's *gundas* were less obvious. I think Balu is working on something more advanced. Much more advanced." Tanuja threw another piece of meat in the water and there was another sickening frenzy.

"I need to get into that lab," Tanuja said as she tossed in the last bit of flesh. This time she didn't wait to see the contest. She turned to face Zilal. With the blood all over their faces and clothes, they were almost black in the moonlight on the riverbank. The apparitions of murdered Indian ladies. To Zilal, it was a conscious but unspoken thought, and then Tanjua manifested it by saying, "I'm going to that funeral tomorrow. I need to get close to Smith to find out what he really knows, and I need to get into that lab."

Zilal nodded. "I think you're crazy," she said, "but I'll do whatever needs doing if it means I can get back into my Red Serge."

13

Dear Tanuja,

I don't know why you have to be so angry just because I forgot which brand of cardamom you like and bought the wrong one. It's my turn to cook anyway, what difference does it make? Did you really need to put a hole in the wall? Some days, it's like you never left your job with the government, and you're still there every day, inside your head. Let's talk about this later. Love you always.

Last written note from Ravneet Mahesh, husband of Tanuja Ramachandran

It was Jaiyana the Librarian and two others: a bruiser named Kamilah, who held the Queens record for having slept with the most number of visiting players; and Naomi, a taciturn Japanese woman with unholy eyes. They had a couple of bottles of gin and one bottle of whiskey between the three of them, all stolen, brazenly, from the bar in Pete Smith's palatial house.

Neither Jaiyana nor Kamilah nor anyone else knew much about Naomi. She'd somehow appeared in Tripoli in 1995, only eighteen years old, and shortly after there'd been a terrorist attack in Tokyo. That and the psychotic twinge in her grin led some of the Nuns to speculate that she'd been in the Japanese cult behind the incident and that she was a key perpetrator in the attack. Either way, Gaddafi had taken her in like he was a vase collector and she was a curiosity that had popped up in a yard sale with an unidentified hairball lodged in her base.

Well, now this middle-aged chipped and cracking vase was at an empty camp ground swilling liquor straight from the bottle with two other women of her ilk. Once they were something. Now they were in the middle of nowhere, holding an impromptu private wake for their fallen comrade, and waiting to be made something again. Something more important than women who prowled the alleys for homeless men and women to abduct, mutilate, and bury.

Jaiyana had seen Balu and Safeera leave Smith's house, so she knew it was safe to sneak out the back way. She grabbed the two nearest co-conspirators she could find, two hunting rifles, and the booze, and off they went – just like Aaliyah the squirrel-eater used to like to do. No one would ever mistake Naomi for a party animal, but tradition dictated that she was off her shift so she had to be invited along. The camp grounds were only open in summer. When they got there,

Kamilah found the generator and powered up some lights, Jaiyana let down her hair and took off her cardigan, and then they started drinking. The ever-present strangeness that emanated from Naomi forced an awkwardness into the situation that Jaiyana and Kamilah could only mitigate by pussy-footing around it and exchanging occasional looks.

The first bottle was almost empty. Naomi had to tip her head almost all the way back to get any out of it, like a seagull. "Come on! Come on! Hurry it up," Kamilah was saying.

"All finished," Naomi said passing her the bottle.

Kamilah tried to take a sip from it anyway, just in case. It was empty. Nothing left but the flavor of gin around the lip. Disappointing. She'd had a third, a whole third of a bottle of gin, but wasn't feeling much of it yet. Ever since they'd started undergoing Balu's treatment it was getting harder and harder to get drunk.

She walked the bottle over to a picnic table about thirty meters away and left it there. Then she came back and gestured to Jaiyana to give her one of the rifles.

She tested the heft of it. "Bullshit," she said pointing at the others. "I used a Vagsta 344 in Libya."

"So did I," said Jaiyana. "We all did. Remember?" Her sardonicism was almost as visible as her breath in the fall air.

Naomi smiled at Kamilah with half her face.

"I destroyed tanks with it," Kamilah continued. "But this thing… this thing is bullshit. What can you kill with this? Deer?" Despite her complaints and her disbelief, she put the rifle up to her shoulder anyway and looked down the sight at the bottle. She took a few breaths, then fired, but after the blast filled the night sky, the bottle was still standing. "Shit! Shit!" she cried. "Goddamn fucking shit!" But she resigned herself to it. "Okay," she said. "Okay." She lowered the gun. "Come on," she said gesturing them to come at her. "Who's first?"

Naomi didn't hesitate. She walked up to Kamilah and threw a punch into her gut on the third step. It wasn't a bad one, but the booze had weakened it a little. She still laughed about it though.

Next Jaiyana walked up and reeled her arm all the way back to punch Kamilah in the face. "Oh, for fuck's sake," Kamilah cursed before the punch connected with her chin.

Jaiyana took the gun from her, and Kamilah got out of the way. She took aim. "Yup," she agreed. "It's no Vagsta." Aaliyah never missed at this game, she thought as she lined up the bottle. Aaliyah would have shot that squirrel. Should have. She pulled the trigger, missed, and sighed. The ritual was repeated only this time Jaiyana was the sucker, and Naomi decided the penalty should be a knee to the crotch.

On Naomi's turn she hit the bottle and it vanished into the night with a crash and echoing cantankerous tinkles. As her reward she gave Kamilah a thunderous slap and tripped Jaiyana so she fell on her ass like a diaper-burdened toddler.

Part way through the second bottle they were starting to feel a bit more sauced. When it was empty, Kamilah stood it on the table as before and took the first shot. Unfortunately, she missed again and suffered for it. Jaiyana was getting creative and gave her some kind of roundhouse kick that missed her head and hit her in the shoulder but still staggered her. It inspired Naomi to do a jump kick too, this one missing completely and she ended up pulling her own thigh. She gave a howl and the other two Nuns laughed.

Naomi hobbled back upright and took a rifle. She didn't even bother aiming, just held the gun at her hip like she was in a Western and blasted away. She took off a chunk of the picnic table, but the bottle was still standing. She hung her head with chagrin. Jaiyana kicked her in her stinging thigh, causing her to wince and hiss through clenched teeth. It was the kind of thing Aaliyah would have done.

Now it was Kamilah's turn. She wanted to do an Aaliyah move on Naomi too, maybe even kick the thigh again, but something made her hesitate. She relaxed her stance but there was still a hint of the belligerence in her voice.

"Tell me something," she said. "Is it true you were in some sort of Japanese cult?"

Jaiyana scoffed. She'd been a Nun for longer than

Kamilah. She knew that Naomi wouldn't answer this question. She would give some sort of weird response that didn't clear up anything.

"Why do you ask me that?" Naomi said.

"Because there are rumors about you."

Kamilah was so much taller than Naomi that Naomi had to look up at her. "No, I mean, why do you ask me that now, here in this picnic place, tonight? Is it because Aaliyah is dead?"

Kamilah looked at Jaiyana. Jaiyana only smiled and shrugged.

"What's the connection?" Kamilah said with lowered eyebrows.

Naomi cracked the cap off the whiskey. "The connection is," she said, "Aaliyah is dead. Now you think about her dead so far from home, for no good reason. And you think, you could be dead too in a few weeks. Why are you here? Going around and around a roller derby track, like we're being stirred in a witch's brew. But you'll never ask yourself that. So you asked me instead."

"I know why I'm here," Kamilah snickered.

Naomi shrugged her eyebrows. "Did you hear who's coming to town? You might be dead the day after tomorrow."

That took both the other women back. "Where did you hear that?" Kamilah asked, trying not to show her consternation.

"Flora."

Kamilah took the gun from Naomi and aimed it at the bottle. Jaiyana took a swig of the whiskey and watched. "I'm here because Banerji is continuing Muammar's mission. Why are you here? Were you in a cult?" she asked again as she lined up the sight.

"Are you a virgin?"

Kamilah fired and missed widely.

"I *was* a virgin," Kamilah muttered loud enough for Jaiyana to hear and laugh.

"Everyone was a virgin," said Naomi.

She reeled her arm back to punch Kamilah in the face. Kamilah caught it as it sped towards her, a violation of the rules so heretical if Aaliyah were here she might have killed Kamilah for it.

"Were you in a cult?"

Naomi flexed her forearm and Kamilah released it. "Did you know that World War III is coming?"

Jaiyana laughed again, but more in surprise this time. Was it about to all come out?

"Nuclear Armageddon? It's there in the teachings. The supreme truth taught by Shiva," Naomi continued.

"And when is this Armageddon going to happen?" Kamilah humored her.

"1997."

Jaiyana laughed so hard she started snorting like a pig.

"Okay," Kamilah said, as if accepting the statement at face value, though Jaiyana's laugh was infectious and she had a wide smile on her face. "Well, it's 2013."

"When I was eighteen, I killed twelve people, to make our leader the new emperor," said Naomi. It didn't answer the 1997 question. "They never caught me. I tried to make Muammar an emperor. Now, Banerji will be Emperor."

The sound of a car and colored lights came from around the road leading into where they were hanging out in the camp grounds among the rental cabins. It was the police. The pasty-faced officer driving pulled up slowly, then stopped and rolled down his window. When he finally got a good look at them and realized he was dealing with members of the town's creepfest roller derby team, he regretting taking the call to investigate the sounds of gunshots.

"You, uh, you ladies out here having some fun, eh?" he said.

Kamilah cocked the gun, raised it with one hand, and shot out his tail light and his false bravado along with it. He immediately drove off again.

When he was gone, Kamilah took the whiskey from Jaiyana and had a guzzle. She pointed the gun at the bottle on the table, one-handed again. "Twelve?" she sneered. "At eighteen? That's nothing."

***

Meanwhile, deep in the woods not far from Pete Smith's mansion, the Monkey Man came limping back to his shack in the woods where his father was waiting. Balu was aghast at the sight of him. His baby was dragging a broken chain and was covered in glass cuts. One of his arms was bent entirely the wrong way. "Oh, my god!" Balu cried, and he caught the Monkey Man as the hairy creature collapsed into his arms.

"She did this to you? That Ramachandran woman? Again?!"

"Dead…" the Monkey man croaked.

Balu nodded, the pride shining through his wet eyes. "Good," he said. In his distraught state, he hardly remembered Safeera.

The Monkey Man managed the energy to point at his own chest. "Last… Starfighter," he rumbled before he passed out. And a tear rolled down Balu's cheek.

14

You ask me: how can a land so renowned for its peace and beauty, the land of passive resistance and Mahatma Gandhi, how could this land have produced Tanuja Ramachandran? Well. India's first nuclear bomb was called the Smiling Buddha.
Lalitha Venkateswaran, Tanuja Ramachandran's *kalaripayattu* trainer

Why did she have to try to eat that squirrel?! Aaliyah hadn't seemed troubled, but in the end she'd snapped and her body… Well, the other women had already bathed it and enshrouded it and the prayers and supplications had already been said. The idea of the burial was too grim to think about. Body in a grave with no casket, and facing Mecca. He accepted that she was dead now. If he'd gotten past the denial, anger, and bargaining, was this now the depression or the acceptance?

Pete phoned down to his assistant to ask him if he owned a funeral suit. Of course he didn't.

***

Down in the lab, deep below the house, he found Balu coming out of the freight elevator pushing a trolley stacked with cardboard boxes. The scientist looked dejected to Pete.

"You're dressed for the funeral, Pete," Balu said, surprised and relieved to see Pete was not wearing another one of those distasteful rock and roll t-shirts.

"What's all this?"

"More research material," Balu said. He stopped the trolley at his work station and started cutting open the boxes. "It arrived yesterday but I was… busy with other things."

Pete looked around the lab. He had furnished Balu with all the latest state-of-the-art equipment. He didn't understand any of it himself, and though he had invested a significant amount of money into setting up the facility for Balu, it was all so futuristic it seemed to be of a cost even beyond what Pete was paying for. And then there was the "No Entry" door in the back corner, where even Pete was not allowed to enter. "Highly sensitive experiments," Balu had told him, and Pete trusted him. Doctor's orders.

"I wish you could come to the funeral too, Mr. Balu," Pete said.

Balu stopped opening the boxes and smiled thinly at Pete. Smith hadn't meant the remark to sound like a master's jab at his slave. He lacked the guile or the malice for that. He genuinely meant it. Pete had a pretty good idea that Balu was wanted by Interpol, and could hardly leave the basement of this house. But he needed a patron and a place to do his research, so here he was.

He's like an idiotic little puppy, Balu thought for the hundredth time.

"Are we getting close?" Pete asked.

"Very close," Balu answered, but he was distracted by the observation that one of the cases looked to have been opened once already and then re-taped shut. He put it into another channel of his mind.

He turned and held Pete by the shoulders. "You have nothing to worry about, Mr. Smith," he said. "We'll have a field test soon. Maybe," he said thinking of what Banerji had told him the day before, "maybe even sooner than you think."

Pete lit up. "Really?"

"Really."

"What's in the boxes?"

Balu looked at him for a moment, thinking (track 1) he really was like a dumb curious animal. At least Pete wasn't as bad all these skaters he thought were going to squeeze his neck until his head popped off, but Balu was still sometimes flabbergasted by the amount of bullshit he had to put up with just so he could continue his research. It was the sorry lot of pure scientists everywhere, especially the greatest of them. Meanwhile on track 2, he remembered his mother. "In this field, the only path to success is to press the flesh," she would always tell him, thinking herself wise in saying it, or maybe she was just resigned to it. She was ultimately killed by a virus Balu had hatched himself in the garage. Track 3 was dedicated entirely to Sabrina's "Boys (Summertime Love)" at the moment.

"*Monomorium santschii*," Balu said with a smile. "More of our ant friends. Maybe our last batch if… things happen. You'll need to give the women another injection tonight. I'll have a set of doses ready for after the funeral. Pete, are you listening to me?"

Pete's brain was sizzling and popping like bacon again. He was almost dizzy with it. "Dr. Balu," he said, "I thought we were making them stronger."

"Of course we are."

"Then what the hell happened to Aaliyah?"

Balu nodded. "I promised you the best skaters on the track, Mr. Smith. The best *legal* skaters, in fact. That I will deliver. But these women, when they dress up in their khakis, they become something else, like primal hunters, jaguars, but machine-like at the same time. Humans have many aspects, Mr. Smith, like diamonds. We're going to turn them into coal again. A state in which the mind is purely at the mercy of physiology. We have had this conversation many times, Mr. Smith."

The supposed logic of it didn't make any sense to Pete. There was going to be a field test soon? With their minds like coal?

On another mental track, Balu was preoccupied with his Monkey Boy, bandaged and shivering in a shack in woods. And yet another track was devoted to Lisa Lisa and Cult Jam.

Pete changed tack. "Mr. Balu, did you know Aaliyah well?"

"I know all my babies well, Mr. Smith. My crazy, crazy babies. And yet, I hardly know them at all…" Balu trailed off in consternation that Pete mistook for grieving.

"I want you to come to the party today. We're going to have a little in memoriam to Aaliyah too. At that goddamn fund raising party. It'll be here at the house, upstairs."

"What?"

"You know. I even had all those gold foil invitations printed up."

"I know about the party, but what do you mean 'in memoriam too'?"

"Same fucking people."

"What?!"

"I mean the same fucking people that were invited to that party will be showing up at what is now also a wake, and pretending to care, and offering underhanded investments for future favors. Me and the skaters are the only ones that that really gave a shit about Aaliyah. And you."

"Of course, Mr. Smith," Balu smiled, though only with his lips. "Of course. I'll be there."

***

The burial took place at Forest Hill Cemetery, the graveyard facing out over the river, Aaliyah facing Mecca, under maple trees with leaves that had turned threatening purples and reds with the season's cold winds. Pete and thirteen women – the skaters – like solid blocks of rage, muscle, and pulsing veins, thirteen Stretch Armstrongs, surrounded the grave, looking down into it with iron frowns. To Pete, even they seemed far away. There were few tears from them, and those seemed to be fighting their way out. Was it the treatment? Was this what it meant to be coal and not diamond? Pete knew the women were different, even back when he first recruited them, but… Hell, Zilal couldn't stop looking around like she was expecting a truant officer to show up, and she kept flexing her jaw and rotating her left shoulder back like she'd messed it up somehow. She was fine at practice yesterday though. But Pete watched her and had to wonder if she even knew where she was. Safeera hadn't come out of her room. Zilal said she was too devastated about the whole thing to participate in the funeral or burial. That made Smith feel better – that one of them felt emotion, and the one he expected would only care about Paris Hilton perfume, no less. But…

Pete started tearing up again, not for Aaliyah, but for his continuing loss of agency, slipping away from him, up into the sky like a helium balloon. The groundskeeper took this as his cue to start shoveling the dirt back into the ground. As the sound of the dirt hitting the shroud reached their ears, the women started to walk away, back down the hill towards the cars.

He finally settled into a labored huffing, mashing his face in his hands like it was play dough, like he was trying to knead out the rage. And then he saw a strange movement in the cluster trees at the edge of the grounds. At first he thought it was the wind, or his imagination, because the colors in motion were the same lavender and carmine as the leaves. And then the movement coalesced into a figure as it came out of the shadows, and it was Tanuja.

Pete trod over the bodies under the grass and past the tombstones, and met her under the leaves, reaching down at them from overhead like the bony suffocating fingers of the winter to come.

"You… you've got some nerve showing up here," he managed to stammer.

"Are you accusing me of something, Mr. Smith?" Tanuja asked, and she held up the crumpled golden ticket he'd given her in the diner less than forty-eight hours before. To Pete, that was a world away now, a world where shit like Galaga mattered, and even Tanuja could see that he was a different man now than he was that night. "You invited me, remember?" Tanuja said.

Her skin seemed to exude a natural perfume of cardamom, turmeric, and saffron. It was so sexual, it affected Pete almost like a knock-out gas. And then there was the line of her neck again, and that midriff, exposed on only one side of her, like a warm, succulent glowing lozenge…

She could see the effect she was having on him, and it was completely intentional of course, but she found it frustrating, almost boring, even angering at the same time. He was so predictable and malleable. And *he* of all people was the third in a triumvirate with Balu and Banerji?

"Listen!" he grunted. "Pretty, pretty dumb of you to be speaking to Sue Wood out in the open like that the night we played the Annihiskaters. That's some stupid shit, lady. And then the same night Aaliyah's dead in pretty goddamn suspicious circumstances, whatever Jane West and Greg Flynn might have to say about it. Jesus! I knew Wood played hardball, but goddamn *murder*?! I don't know why the hell you're still in town, but I'm glad you decided to stick around. I'm going to find all the proof I need on you."

"I don't know who Sue Wood is," Tanuja said. "If you mean that hobbit from the parking lot, she accosted me and accused me of being a ringer on your team. If anything, I'm the one that needs to be asking you the questions, Mr. Smith."

Maybe it was the Acapulco Gold he'd smoked in the car, but she said it with such uniform conviction that he believed it. And in the same instant another thought dawned on him, though maybe that was the Acapulco too.

"Oh, shit. The Women's Flat Track Derby Association sent you, didn't they…"

"Mr. Smith…"

"I went through all this with you people last year! Everything's above board. No restricted substances, I swear. You can test the ladies. Why the fuck would the WFTDA want Aaliyah dead?!"

She slapped him full in the face like he was a Windows XP machine that had gone full blue — *dishum!* – then grabbed him by the shoulders.

"I want none of those things, Mr. Smith. Like I told you, I'm just passing through town." Her grip on his shoulders loosened. She could see in his eyes that the death of Aaliyah had affected him, but she processed this as mere datum, like a computer would. There was no actual sympathy from her, just a line of sight, like an arrow-straight trail of fire in the night that roared towards Balu.

But Pete Smith deflated with a sigh, and succumbed to her faux compassion. Who else could he turn to? Even the Qarnage Queens had been acting so strange lately. With some of them, it was almost like their minds had been taken over. They were almost unrecognizable. And Sheriff Flynn was trying to blame him for all sorts of things…

"You know," Pete said, "with this jerk off epidemic going on, you'd better keep an eye on your brother. Seems to me he might be especially vulnerable."

"Max doesn't need a viral pathogen to encourage

that sort of behavior." He was sensitive to certain types of smells though. "He's safely locked away anyway. But now you tell me, Mr. Smith, why ever would you be worried about someone accusing you of cheating? After I saw the game the other night, I became very interested. There's really so much more I would like to know about roller derby, and you're the one to explain it to me, aren't you?"

He clenched his jaw and held his breath for a moment. Then he said, "You know what? There's something I want to show you."

***

Pete drove Tanuja out to Grand Lake Meadow. On the way, she tried to make small talk with him to make herself seem normal, but all she could come up with was sitar music. She tried to explain to him about the masters like Bhimsen Joshi and Annapurna Devi, but it was a bit like talking to your dog about the day you had at work. But he kind of understood since he liked fast guitar playing and talked about bands with grammatically incorrect names like Megadeth and DragonForce. Tanuja's brain rubber stamped the conversation: "SATISFACTORY."

When they got to the park, he parked his car at the edge of the woods where the walking trails began. "Why, Mr. Smith, I hardly know you," she said as they started heading towards the path. Coming from Tanuja, it sounded about as flirtatious as a shark eating a license plate, but Pete chuckled anyway.

"Trust me," he said. "It's totally safe. I know there's been some stuff about bobcats in the news lately, but I don't buy that shit for a second. It's just an excuse…" He stopped himself short.

"An excuse for what?" she pushed him.

They were under the canopy of trees now and the fading sun came through in dappled patches. The dirt path was littered with dry, crunchy purple and red leaves.

"The disappearances. Some people disappearing in Fredericton lately. You might have heard about it."

"No," she lied, "but why isn't it national news?"

Pete shrugged. "Apparently, it's only homeless people. This town is full of rich assholes. If any one of them or their families went missing, it would be another story. As it is, right now *you* probably know more about the disappearances than they do."

Tanuja wondered if it was it possible he really knew nothing about them, or whether he was testing her knowledge. He certainly sounded genuine though. "I'm guessing *you're* rich, Mr. Smith."

He nodded. "I'm probably an asshole too. That sari doesn't look cheap either though." He was right. Even in this dim light, the gold thread caught the sun and reflected it back like polished armor. "You sure you want to be walking in the woods with it?"

"I'm fine."

"We're almost there."

"You still haven't told me where we're going, Mr. Smith."

Before he could answer, a jogger came up from behind, passed them, then after a few more paces stopped and swiveled back, pointing a black revolver at them.

"Wallet. Purse," he said. His shorts were too short and too tight. You could make out the outline of his dick. Tanuja wouldn't have been surprised if his headband had already caught the attention of Olivia Newton John's lawyers.

Tanuja didn't move. Pete put up his hands and said, "Easy there, pal. You can have our stuff, okay. There's no –"

Tanuja interjected. "*Dey*! That's a Raskog .22. You're seven meters away." Pete was looking at her wide eyed. "Even if you hit anything, do you think it will even go through my blouse?"

The jogger's face had gone pale and constricted, but he found his courage again in the form of anger that flushed his face again, and he started walking right up to her. "Is this close enough for ya?" he said.

It was close enough for her. She kicked the hand brandishing the gun, then, while it was airborne kicked him in the nuts, then caught the gun, and smashed his nose with the butt of the handle like it was a pestle and she was using it to grind blood-soaked tamarind powder in his face.

The jogger staggered back with an anguished cry,

holding his nose and blinded by blood and pain. Tanuja stepped over to the edge of the path and tested the heft of a few fallen tree branches before finding one about as big around as her arm that satisfied her. She swung it in the air like a bat a few times, then walked over to the jogger and knocked him out with it. Pete had remained frozen where he was standing the whole time, but the sound of the crunch alone was enough to make him feel a wave of nausea. He'd seen his share of shattered bones and joints on the track, but this…

Tanuja pulled the jogger over to the side of the path so no one tripped over him. If she weren't undercover, she wouldn't have gone so easy on him.

"Where did… where did you learn to do that?" Pete asked.

"Lacrosse," she said.

***

"This is it," Pete said. They had arrived at a cabin, accessible only by foot, that must have been hundreds of years old, or at least maintained such that it still looked that way. The grounds were highlighted with pretty, well-tended flower beds, which, even now in the fall, dazzled with blue-stars, rosy asters, and chrysanthemums. The grass was immaculate, and still a spring green. There was the hum of a generator hidden cleverly somewhere. If Tanuja had still had a living soul within her, she would have been charmed. As it was, she could only process the visual data and give a simulacrum's smile in response.

"I imagined you lived somewhere grander, Mr. Smith," she said. "Is this your summer home?"

"It's much more than that," he said as they walked up the gravel path to the front door. Pete unlocked it and let Tanuja go in ahead of him.

Inside, it somehow seemed larger, but cozy and warm at the same time. "This cottage," Pete said as Tanuja walked around, "was once owned by Laura Secord."

"Really?"

"Canada's premier chocolatier," he continued. Indeed, even now, two hundred years after Laura Secord's heyday, it still smelled like chocolate. He indicated she should have a seat on the couch. He went into the kitchenette and got them drinks out of the fridge while he talked. "And also – though very few people know this – she was also the woman who invented roller derby back in 1797 when she was only twenty-two years old. Although back then they played on ice skates, of course, just a few kilometers from here on the Saint John River."

"I didn't realize roller derby was a Canadian invention," Tanuja said from the fur-covered sofa.

He handed her a bottle of Moosehead and went to light the fireplace. "Uh huh," he said. "Just like basketball, egg cartons, and Loverboy." He got the fire going soon enough, but it was sputtering and sickly. He stayed beside it, staring into it, like he was trapped between it and the invisible black fog aura that surrounded the woman he'd brought here. "That thing back there," he said without looking at her. "That wasn't lacrosse, was it?

"Mr. Smith, you didn't ask if I wanted a drink, and you didn't ask if I was cold, and, yet, here I am with a beer in my hand at five in the afternoon in front of a fire in Laura Secord's cabin, and you're asking me about lacrosse." The silk threads of her sari glittered in the firelight, otherworldly and beautiful, but inside her her mind was buzzing with termites. What was she supposed to say? How was she supposed to act? She was here in this room, what some humans would call a "romantic" cabin, but to her she might as well have been looking at a picture of a switch track lever in Rail Enthusiast Monthly. She had to pull the words to say from the faint memories of serials she'd read all the way back in the orphanage days. She caught herself sitting forward with arms on her knees, poised for a forward leap, and had to force herself into a more relaxed position leaning back against the fur cover. Now more than ever she wished she could be staring into her kaleidoscope or that the Rani would show up with advice.

But then it started to come out. "No, it wasn't lacrosse," she said. "I grew up in Pondicherry, a city in south India which was occupied by the French until 1954, several years after the British had left. My maternal grandfather was a Spitfire pilot in The Battle of Britain. When I was nine and my brother was six, our parents were killed, murdered."

"Holy shit."

"We were put in an orphanage. As you can probably imagine, the orphanage was not good. It was less an institution than an earthen structure where the children cleaned and worked and died while the sand blew in off the street. But after a year or two or a thousand in this place, one day some government men came. Hard looking men in khaki uniforms. Recruiters, looking for children to train, to turn into weapons they could wield. I had seen my parents' bodies, and even then I knew these men were from that same shadow world. I don't know how they chose me. I suppose they knew what to look for. I suppose perhaps we are born the way we are supposed to be, and they knew how to recognize it. I do not know if those of us they selected had any say in the matter, but at first they didn't act like we had to go with them. They took us away from the home, into the city to buy things. They said we could buy one of anything we wanted. They promised there would be more if we went with them. This was a seduction. Even when I was ten, I knew it. Something in me knew what would happen if I went with them, through that door to the shadow side. And that same thing told me that I was *supposed* to go through it. It was what I was meant to do. So I went to the shops and the parks that day like they expected of me. And at the end of the day, when it was time to get in their jeeps to go through the portal into the shadow lands, I said, 'No.' One of them grabbed me, and I broke his arm in a way my mother had taught me. I said I would go with them but only if I could have assurances my brother would be put in a good home and well taken care of. I broke the man's fingers and they agreed. And then they taught me to… play lacrosse. Day after day, for hours on end, until each day my skin felt like bark and my muscles turned to tree trunks. For years. I was ten years old. And I played their lacrosse games for them until I was twenty-one. After that, when I was still so young, I tried to have a normal life, for a time. That was taken from me too."

"So… what was the thing you bought?"

"A comic book about Lakshmibai, the Rani of Jhansi."

"Who?"

"She was an Indian queen. She rode her horse into battle against the British, probably not too long after your Laura Secord invented her chocolate and roller derby." Tanuja took a swig of beer.

Pete remained standing at the mantel. "I want you to skate for me," he said.

She scoffed through her nose. "I told you, Mr. Smith, I'm just passing through. Is this how you recruit all your skaters?"

"No, they, you know…" Pete's voice trailed off and he became hypnotized by the fire. "You know, I hardly knew that woman we buried today. I only thought I did. Her name was Aaliyah."

"So how did she join your team?"

"Well, a couple of years back, all my skaters just started getting headhunted all at once into other teams. It seemed suspicious at the time, but suspicious of what? It wasn't like it was just one team scooping them up. Anyway, it gave me the chance to start over, and right about this same time, I met this man. I guess you could say he's sort of a..." He gave Tanuja a somewhat guilty look, and mumbled, "a sports doctor. And he said he knew some women that would be keen to learn to skate and would be willing to move to Fredericton. And Aaliyah was one of them."

"And what did this sports doctor want in return?" Tanuja asked.

"Why would you assume..." he began, but then her cold stare told him that she'd already connected the dots. "He wanted financing for his research. It's mutually beneficial."

"But it's not cheating."

He mustered an ironic laugh. "Right," he said, "it's not cheating. But it's not fair either. If the Flat Track Association knew about it, they would ban it. I never meant for it to be this way. In didn't know he would go this far, but it's not like any of the skaters are complaining. Things are just getting out control. Out of *my* control. Sometimes it feels like it's affecting the whole town. I spend half the time trying to convince the city sheriff he's got nothing to worry about, and the other half trying to convince myself. He gives me the benefit of the doubt because I own half the businesses in town. But I've got no reason to trust *myself*." The crackling fire transfixed his gaze again.

Tanuja sensed that he wasn't going to reveal anything about the lab despite the guilt he was puking out. That didn't matter. She needed to get as close to him as possible, make him trust her again, so she could get into his house, past the guards and bulletproof glass, and make her own way to the lab as she had planned with Zilal.

"But you went along with it for the sake of the sport," she stated.

He nodded. "I realize how dumb my fixation must seem. I hear the way other people talk about paintings or murder mysteries and I wonder what they see in it. But it wasn't always this way. My parents established the area roller derby league, and then they died within a year of each other when I was seventeen. And mom died in the most awful way, in a hospital bed, almost unrecognizable. And she could barely speak, but last words she said to me were 'roller derby.' And I don't know why she said that really, but I believe it was because she wanted me to carry on her legacy. So I was left alone with our dog Kirby, but he was getting older and died too. But after she said that, all the pieces fell into place for me, and I saw how the sport was tied to life and the universe by some sort of ley lines. I don't really know what else to do with that money. That house is still pretty much just the way they left it." (*Except for the lab in the basement*, Tanuja thought.) "I can't bear to change it," he continued. "But did *they* even care about any of that stuff though? I mean, her last words to me were 'roller derby!'"

She could barely speak, Tanuja thought. *Roller derby... Older Kirby... Nnnooo, it couldn't be... could it?* But even if his mother really had said "roller derby," Tanuja realized in that moment that every piece on the board, including herself, was a porcelain sculpture that had shattered and been put back together by a universe with the mind of an imbecile using scotch tape and school glue. The piece that was Pete Smith had been put back together and labelled "PATSY."

"And if I did decide to join your team, Mr. Smith, even though I can't, would I be subjected to this research as well?"

"Well..."

"And what about your ulterior motive for taking all these untested skaters on at the same time?" She stood up and walked over to within a few feet of him. "We barely know each other, Mr. Smith, but I know how important this roller derby business is to you, and I have trouble believing you would be willing to bring so many green skaters on board at once."

"Well, the research would..."

"Were you having sex with them?"

He knew she was going to say it, but it still stung.

She continued before he could interject. "Are you having sex with Flora? You seem close." She grabbed his shoulder and pushed it just enough to make him stumble back a step against the mantel.

"No," he protested, "no." The guilt in his eyes said he wanted to though. "They're… not like ordinary women. They seem beholden to some higher ideal." Or a higher person, Tanuja thought. "And especially after the treatments started…" he tried to continue. He half laughed again, but it was mirthless. "I just don't get them. You know the doctor once told me that women like romance and orgasms and are repulsed by everything in between."

Tanuja slapped him – *dishum!* – then grabbed his pasty Caucasian jaw like she was inspecting a broken carburetor. "I couldn't give a shit about romance, Mr. Smith," she said.

Down at the end of the line of her arm, he saw that perfect brown square of exposed flesh between her sari blouse and her waist. And peeking out from the edge of the blouse, the final trails of a craggy topographical purplish scar. He tossed his beer bottle into the fire and it atomized into a million stars. She kissed him, deeply, and flung him onto the couch. She had his belt off and was whipping him with it before he knew what was going on. And, when all was said and done, he turned out to be a fairly decent lay.

15

Interviewer: I don't want you to get the false impression that you're here only because of your language skills. This could be a long assignment, deep cover. Penetrating Gaddafi's organization will require a fortitude the likes of which you never had call to draw upon in the RCMP.
Zilal al-Thani: You had me at "penetrating Gaddafi."
CSIS candidate interviews, 2006

As they pulled into the driveway of Smith's mansion, it seemed to Tanuja that the party was more like an Asshole of the Year pageant than any show of mourning and minus any talent competition that might have redeemed it. The worst of Fredericton's privileged wealthy, old and new, turned up in a string of limos that kept the elm trees company all the way up the street. The men wore jackets and no ties like they were "hip," and had faces so pale and oily Tanuja wanted to wipe them in a pan and fry up an egg. The women looked like they'd carried out a strike force assault and recovery on Vanna White's wardrobe circa 1987. Half the attendees were trophies, the other half were boy toys. Unlike what might be found in other cities, though, it was quite racially varied, full of Asians, subcontinentals, Africans, Arabs, and South Americans.

Pete parked the car and stepped out. Tanuja followed out the passenger side. Flora was standing there waiting for them.

"What's she doing here?" she asked with all the personality of a game of Pong.

"I, uh, invited her."

"You invited her to Aaliyah's wake?!"

"No, to the party, remember? Look, she just wants to pay her respects. Is having her here any worse than the rest of these yahoos?" he said, nodding around.

As if on cue, a white man with silver hair walked up and shook Pete's hand. The woman with him looked like she'd come out of a 3D printer. "Sorry to hear about the Middle Eastern bird, Pete," the man said, "I know all that ice skating business means a lot to you."

His lady friend laughed so hard she snorted, and a puff of spilled or forgotten cocaine billowed off her Barbie cleavage.

"Yeah, thanks, Jack. Hello, Belle," Pete said to the woman with him.

"Hey, who's your lady friend, Pete? Is she… Hey, is she asleep?"

Tanuja was indeed sprawled across Pete's Bricklin from the waist up.

"I'll see you inside, okay, Jack?" Pete allowed.

The man left with a smile. Belle stumbled, almost fell but found her footing, and then barfed on her Louboutins.

"I, uh, I think you should go in too, Flora," Pete said.

"But –"

"Please?"

Flora turned and the gravel crunched under her boots as she walked away.

Pete sighed.

"Am I a 'yahoo,' Mr. Smith?" Tanuja asked Pete, straightening out her sari.

"I'm not sure if that's the word for it, but I'd say one of your skates has popped a wheel loose at least." He smiled, and she took this as a sign that he considered this post-coital lovers' banter. "You probably met some of these people in the VIP booth," he continued. "They'll talk about roller derby, but none of them really care about it. They just think that by showing up there or here they can impress me and get at my mom and dad's money. But you… this isn't really your scene, is it? You actually agreed to come here – you wanted to come here – of your own free will."

"You're the one that invited me, Mr. Smith."

"And you're still the one that might get me through this thing."

Inside the mansion, in the main ballroom, there was a blown up picture of Aaliyah skating on a roller derby track hanging from the wall and an altar with flowers placed in front of it. There was no other indication that someone had died two days earlier. People bustled and danced and drank, and caterers mingled through the crowd carrying trays piled with hors d'oeuvres that looked like refuse salvaged from a jungle floor and speared with toothpicks. There was hardly room to move, and the cloud of hair spray fumes almost made Tanuja dizzy. Pete didn't look too happy either, but as soon as he entered the room he was immediately approached by Greg Flynn, the sheriff, shifting his feet and huffing through his nose. Seeing Tanuja standing next to Pete, he hesitated, but only for a moment. He was ready to cut loose.

"Not now, Greg," Pete said.

"Goddamn it, Pete! There's a parade happening *tomorrow* and people in this town are jerking off like crazy!"

"I know! Those people worked for me, remember? I've got more important things to worry about now than the damn la-di-dah parade, Greg."

It was unusual to Tanuja that Flynn would be so concerned about the masturbators ruining a small town parade, or that the former could even affect the latter. "What's so special about this parade?" she asked.

Pete didn't answer her, but continued speaking to Flynn. "I know how important the parade is."

"This is bigger than the parade. These past few months… things have been getting weird, and it's got something to do with *you* and the skaters and that cinema downtown. You don't need to admit it, the look on your face tells me you agree with every word of it. I am losing control of this city, you bastard!"

They were interrupted by a man in a black suit, wearing sunglasses, and an electronic earpiece. "Mr. Smith," he said, "the PM is ready." Pete nodded and the man left.

"The PM?" Tanuja said. "He's *here*? Tonight? But there was wasn't even a security check at the door?"

"You see!" Flynn said to her, veins straining in his forehead. "Just think about what it's going to be like at the parade tomorrow!" She stared at him to continue. "He's going to be *at* the parade!"

Flynn stormed off.

"Excuse me," Pete said to Tanuja. He went up to the podium and had to ring a champagne glass with a fork, like it was a goddamn wedding, to get everyone to quiet down and listen to him. He looked out over the sea of faces. No, not a sea. More like a trough full of soil-encrusted, lumpy mushrooms bedecked with sequins and toupees that looked to be on the verge of escape. The catering staff continued to circulate. In the near silence, someone farted.

"Look, guys," he started. "Aaliyah's teammates knew her better than I ever could, but I want to say some things about her before we get to the main event.

She was a wicked ass jammer. The best. I don't know why she had to die so damn young. I guess all we can do is keep skating."

"Do 'Freebird!'" somebody shouted, and everybody laughed. Pete heard Belle snort again.

"Very funny, Steve," Pete said, and gave up. "Well. Enjoy the champagne, I guess. We all know who you jerks are really here for. Ladies and gentlemen, the Prime Minister of Canada."

As the PM walked onto the stage and shook Pete's hand, his face was oblivious to Pete's almost nihilistic indifference.

***

The Prime Minister was known for his Caucasian good looks and being so liberal it was almost reactionary. Aldous Chretien had been born into a long political dynasty, and was the son of a former long-serving PM. His teeth were immaculate. He gave a rousing speech, and left the stage to raucous applause aimed at Aaliyah's blown up photo on the wall.

Tanuja was over by the hors d'oeuvres table waiting for the opportunity to rendezvous with Zilal, and lining up a row of three samosas on her plate in a perfect line. A man beside her, who had been humming Eddie Murphy's "Party All the Time" and piling his own plate without ever looking at hers, said, "You know those are beef samosas, right?"

Tanuja turned and looked at him. He was an

Indian man (his accent had announced that) with brushed hair and a trimmed goatee. He still wasn't looking at her.

"I eat beef," she said.

"Good," he said, perusing the cheeses. "So do I. I don't go in for any nonsensical religious dictates."

He didn't say it like he was making small talk. He declared it, almost yelped it.

He glanced over at her plate, saw the samosas in a perfect line, then moved his gaze up her violet and crimson sari to her face and eyes.

It was astonishing. On the surface, she looked like a functioning, adjusted member of this idiotic society. She probably had everyone at this party fooled into thinking she was just like any of them. And yet, there was a certain flash in her eyes, the tension of the skull beneath the skin, the flawless line of samosas. Doctor Balu knew that she was almost certainly a carrier of the MAOA gene: resulting in too much serotonin being released into her brain in utero, and insensitivity to the neurotransmitter later in life. She was probably sociopathic, maybe a psychopath too. God! How Balu wished he could perform a PET scan on her brain, EEGs, MRIs – the whole battery. What a remarkable specimen she would be!

"Are you… are you one of Mr. Smith's business partners?" he asked, but in the same instant his mind split off onto three other tracks.

Track 1: Assuming the presence of the gene, was

there a trauma witnessed or involved in, pre-puberty which triggered psychopathology? He started working on the scenarios. The murder of a relative while the subject was a youth could do it.

Track 2: Was it too late to adjust the neurotransmitter inhibitors in the skaters' nightly dosage? The parade was tomorrow. They would only have tonight's course of injections. What he wouldn't give for a sample of this woman's blood!

Track 3: Whatever happened to Rednex? Did they make enough money off of "Cotton Eye Joe" in the nineties to survive into 2017? Or were they stealing scrap copper to sell for meth before their inevitable suicides?

This entire thought process took less than half a second.

"No," she answered. Then she spotted Zilal across the room and said, "Excuse me, I need to take out my diaphragm," and walked away.

Watching her leave, another thought occurred to him. Could it be *her*? But she was dead. And, certainly this woman's gymnastic musculature was conspicuous, but she was about the least erotic woman Balu had ever seen, even if she *was* wearing a diaphragm. She was an anti-matter dimension manifestation of coquettishness. Still… He wanted to go down to the lab, but was accosted by another Indian couple who insisted on making conversation.

***

Zilal was in a corner, scowling and dressed in khaki fatigues like the other skaters who were "on duty." "Fuck these people," she said to the universe as Tanuja approached.

"Well?" Tanuja asked. She spoke to her samosas and faced away from Zilal.

"Took your sweet fucking time. Where's your brother?"

"Not far. In the car on a side street waiting in case I need him."

"You know, I saw you at the graveyard. Talking to Pete in the shadows of the leaves, but you were right there out in the open. Then when I turned around, I saw Flora down in the parking lot watching *me*. This whole thing stinks worse than the fish market in Tripoli before they started selling bullets there."

"Can we get on with it?" Tanuja said.

"Fine," Zilal replied. "Let's go over it again. Shift change in about two minutes. You're going to see a woman called Jaiyana come around the corner of that hall you can see just past the big doors into this room. You'll recognize her. She'll have a vest, a bun in her hair, a chain on her glasses, and you'll be afraid she's going to charge you late fees on an overdue copy of *Huckleberry Finn*."

"I remember," Tanuja replied. She glanced over her shoulder and saw the hallway Zilal meant. It was bathed in bright, yellow light from chandeliers.

"You'll need to follow her," Zilal continued. "But

once she executes the unlock sequence the access elevator doors will only be open for about ten seconds before they go into lock down mode again."

"*Dey! I remember*," Tanuja hissed again.

"Good. Once you get down in the lab, there must be another access point for deliveries. And based on the patterns I've observed, sometimes people seem to go down but not come back up again."

Tanuja looked across at the yellow-lit hallway again, when a middle-aged overly-tanned man came up behind her and said, "What's a nice –"

She whacked him on the side of the head like it was a *tabla*, kneed him in the stomach so he doubled over, then spun him around and shoved him back into the throng unnoticed.

Zilal's lips went into a line. "Maybe I should be the one to go down there," she said.

"Why break your cover now? We talked about this last night."

Out of the corner of her eye, she spotted the librarian, Jaiyana, go around the corner and down the hall.

Zilal nodded. "You better get your fucking ass in gear."

Tanuja nodded back and wasted no time hustling off into the vase-lined hall. Smith hadn't changed any of the furnishings in the house after his parents died, just like he'd said. None of it suited him. For a fraction of a second, she was distracted by an Alex Colville painting on the wall of a dark horse charging towards a black locomotive with one cyclopean headlight in the dusk, then she scurried away again, her sari swishing with military regularity. For a second it looked like the Rani was on that horse, but she disappeared after a blink.

Tanuja followed Jaiyana around a corner, down a staff staircase, through the service kitchen, then down a dim hall, far from the crowds and empty save for the two of them. Several feet ahead of her, Jaiyana stopped in front of closed steel door. Tanuja ducked behind a corner. Jaiyana adjusted her glasses and unlocked the door with a key on a chain around her neck, then went into the room and closed the door behind her. Tanuja slid up and listened at the door, slipping her brass knuckles out of her purse.

There was a series of noises: something solid and heavy being shifted aside, typing on a keyboard, the jingle of the keys on the chain around her neck, the click of the key, the shunt of an elevator door opening.

That was her cue.

Tanuja kicked the door open, saw the woman standing in front of the elevator door, then kicked the woman. Jaiyana stumbled backwards, and managed to find her feet in time to dodge a punch that swooshed past her ear, and land a punch of inhuman strength into Tanuja's midriff in the same motion. That gave Jaiyana a breath to land another punch right in Tanuja's jaw. She was fast. But perhaps cautious too:

instead of pressing her advantage, she backed up, too far to reach. Tanuja used the instant to take in her surroundings. A dark, dingy office. A cluttered desk at one end. The freight elevator doors started to close, but the librarian was edging back towards the desk, deliberately, like she was going to go for a panic button. For a moment, they eyed each other. Tanuja heard the elevator doors slide shut behind her. Jaiyana reached for the desk, her arm snapping out like a lizard's tongue, faster than humanly possible, but it was a miscalculation. Tanuja lunged in the same instant, pinned the arm with a *silambam* lock, snapped it, and cut her cry short with a brass knuckle hammer-blow to the temple that knocked her to the floor. The effort of the punch had drained her breath, but she yanked the necklace with the key from Jaiyana's neck and wiped the blood from her lip. When she turned to the elevator, Pete Smith was standing there in the office doorway, gazing at the floor like he had x-ray eyes and was scanning the core of the Earth for kidney stones.

"I knew it," he muttered as if speaking to the kidney stones. "I knew it. You *are* working for Sue Wood. You're a goddamn spy." His voice was still quiet. He could be as harmless as he seemed, or a roller derby infraction could be the thing that made him snap. It was hard for Tanuja to tell in that moment, but he had his hands in his hair in distress and was unarmed.

"I'm not working for Sue Wood," she said.

"Bullshit," he said, looking at Jaiyana, not Tanuja, with tears welling up in his eyes, "You… you're the fucking one that killed Aaliyah! Did you beat up my projectionist too? And this afternoon, that was all bullshit too." He finally looked at her.

"No." She said, half truthfully, though indeed she had played him like a *veena*. "It was true."

He went on, as though she hadn't spoken. "I opened up to you. About the skaters and my parents and my dog! And you felt nothing."

He was all over the map, but she answered him. "No," she said, "I felt something." And she sort of meant it.

They looked at each other for a moment until she spoke.

She straightened up. "Pete, I'm going to tell you some things and some of them aren't going to make sense to you, but you're going to have to keep quiet and hear me out and believe all of it. I'm a mercenary." He almost said something, then remembered her admonition. "I've been hired by the government of India, off the books. Your sports doctor is a man named Srikanth Balu. Yes, I know that. But he's not working for you. He's working for a terrorist named Banerji." Now his mouth flapped like a fish's. "Your skaters are all ex-Revolutionary Nuns, Gaddafi's personal virgin guard."

"What?!"

"I said to keep quiet. Balu is genetically modifying them into killing machines. He can do it. In 2001 he created a half-human, half-monkey thing that I thought I killed, but it's still alive and it's here, somewhere, in Fredericton." At this, his face contorted every which way. "And probably as soon as those women are ready, they'll go straight into Banerji's army. Neither of them give a shit about you or your roller derby. They're using you. And, yes, you better believe I killed Aaliyah. She was hardly human any more. None of them are. Last night I killed Safeera too. Now I need to get down into that lab and shut this shit down. P.S. You've got the Prime Minister of the country upstairs. Even if I slept with you just so I could get this far, you should be grateful."

"… Can we go back to saying you were a lacrosse player?" he said.

"Yes," she answered, "if you'll open those elevator doors."

He walked over to the desk and punched some numbers into a keyboard amidst the clutter. The elevator hummed awake again. Then he walked over to her, took the key, put it into a keyhole by the elevator call button, turned it, and the doors opened again. Then, to her surprise, he went straight into it and put his hand on the door to keep it open for her.

"What are you doing?" she said.

Pete cleared his throat. "Something was wrong. I've had a bad feeling, in my stomach, for ages. Of course I did. They aren't like my old team. But if something bad's happening to them… I'm responsible. I need to know what's really going on down there."

"What about your party?"

"As if any of them cared that I was even there in the first place."

She got in and he let the doors close. They were silent as the elevator started its descent.

He said, with a dry, suppressed quiver in his voice, "Did you say… half-monkey, half-man?"

"Yes," she said, looking at the elevator doors. "With a hole clear through its chest. Smells like shit. Been wearing the same shirt since 2001."

"Enjoys the outdoors, meeting new people, long walks on the beach."

She looked at him and one side of her lip edged upwards so slightly that only the LIGO gravitational wave detector could have measured it. By her standards, it may have been the equivalent of a smile.

The elevator came to a juddering stop, the doors started to open onto the darkness of the lab, and there was a Nun there waiting for the shift change with a machinegun slung over her shoulder. "What took you so —" she started to say before she realized it was not Jaiyana. It was Pete Smith and some woman in a sari. The machine gun was up and aimed with no apparent intermediate movement, like the quantum leap of an electron, but just as quickly the strap was cinched hard around her neck. Smith yelled, "Deenah!" and the woman's eyes began to roll… Pete Smith watched it happen with a dumbstruck expression on his face. Tanuja was straining like she was trying to pull the head off the Venus de Milo. In her flailing, Deenah flipped and kicked a stainless steel lab station crumpling the corner of it before Tanuja wrenched her back around again and she finally sank like a crash test dummy. Tanuja looked up at Pete, a bead of sweat streaming down her forehead, her eyes wide, as if to say, *You see?* His mouth flattened into a line of *I know*.

She scanned the lab. The equipment on display beggared belief, but of course it would have to. "Tell me what I need to know," she said.

"Okay," he said. "Over this way."

He led her to a man-sized cabinet with a glass door. The cabinet was filled with vials. "These are the ones he's working on. When they're ready – these ones with the red stickers – Dr. Balu gives me a case to take upstairs and inject the skaters with. There's a certain schedule and rotation. I don't really understand it."

"You just do it," she said with disgust plain on her face.

"Yeah," he said, "Although… sometimes they give me this look, hostile, crazy if there's even a hint that maybe we ought to slow down."

"Is that his desk?" she said pointing to a corner.

"Yes."

She went over to it, lifted the PC up off the floor, swung it overhead in a huge arc, and smashed it against the ground, twice. The second time the casing gave and the contents spilled out like she'd gutted a robot. She jerked out the hard drive, slammed it on the desk, pulled a gun out her purse and blasted it, lighting up the lab for an instant.

"What's through that door?" she said, jabbing her chin at the opposite corner of the room.

"I've never been in there," he said with embarrassment in his voice. "Off limits, even to me." Even he was aware of how naïve he sounded.

She swapped her pistol for her *kattari* dagger and crossed to the door, and Pete kept up behind her like a faithful dog. She jammed the *kattari* into the locking mechanism and shredded it open. When she swung the door open, a putrid stench wafted out of the darkness so foul she had to cover her nose with her sari. It was accompanied by weak animalistic moans. Tanuja groped and found a light switch, and the scene that came into view was horrific. The room was effectively an extension of the lab, antiseptic and clean, with more equipment, but there were two rows of cages down each side, five to a wall, most occupied by what appeared to be listless and defeated derelicts. They had been in darkness, but most seemed awake. When the lights came on some of them scrambled to the front of their cages and started rattling the bars and howling like Tanuja and Pete were fresh meat. Some of them, though, were sat on the floor in their corners staring at nothing and never budged, catatonic. None of them looked well. They had rough skin, knotted hair. It was easy to see at a glance that they had been Fredericton's homeless. And despite their wearing clean hospital gowns, they looked like they hadn't bathed or shaved for days. No – they weren't unshaven. They were inhumanly hairy, even the women. Tanuja remembered the men she fought in the mannequin factory. Some of these people were further along.

"Holy shit," she heard Pete say behind her as he surveyed the room.

A second after the angry howling started, it shifted to stunned curiosity. These weren't the usual people who came in here.

Near the front of the lab, there was another cabinet with boxes of vials. Tanuja opened the cabinet and went through one of the boxes. The vials had the same color scheme.

Pete was at the other end of the room tugging on the steel back door, but it was locked. "We need to find some keys," he said.

Tanuja started to cross the room to him, when one of the prisoners jumped up at the sight of her and started making happy noises. The noise caught Pete's attention too.

"Bolo?" Tanuja said stopping in front of his cage. It was him. The big man reached through the bars and touched her face gently and gratefully. A tear streamed down his cheek. "My stink," he muttered. This set off the other conscious prisoners, who reached through the bars to try to lay hands on their savior too.

"Okay," she said.

She angled her *kattari* into the lock and then froze solid, like she'd heard something in the distance.

"What?" Pete said.

She abandoned the lock and walked over to him. "Turn around and drop your pants," she said.

"What?"

She forced him around and yanked his pants down. There was a half dead cheer from one of the cages. He felt a needle sting in his ass. "What the fuck?!" he said hauling his pants up.

But when he turned around, Banerji and Balu were standing in the doorway backed up by a crew of Gaddafi's khaki-garbed women with machineguns.

16

Like pouring ghee into fire.
Tamil proverb

Max had been parked a few blocks from Pete Smith's mansion peacefully eating his Kraft macaroni out of a *tiffin* carrier. But from the moment the two paramilitary roller derby skaters yanked him out of it, spilling his meal everywhere, to when they shoved him stumbling into the back of the van, all he could think was, "Why did I have to sniff those bicycle seats?"

Because doing so had got him kicked out of vet college, then, the second time, tarnished his reputation at the embassy and scuttled his rising career, so that now here he was with his hands tied and surely about to be driven to his execution.

No – that wasn't exactly accurate. The incident itself wasn't the problem: he'd been habitually smelling ladies' bicycle seats for months; the issue was that he'd been caught. And his reputation hadn't been "tarnished": it had been cemented. In his darkest moments, he felt that the sum total quality of the world would be better without perverts like him in it: better that they were plucked out of it entirely. He started humming a tune, but a Nun whacked him on the side of the head.

In any case, the scandal led to a demotion and a career on an alternate track of essentially meaningless positions within the embassy. And that, somehow, had led him here.

But then he saw his sister and Pete Smith in the van too, tied up like him and sat on benches that had been installed lengthwise along each wall as makeshift troop transport. The two women shoved Max down onto the bench opposite her.

Tanuja's eyes widened to see him captured, but her surprise soon turned into a rictus toothy grimace set against a bruised face and disheveled hair. Smith looked beat up too, but he only gave Max's arrival the barest glance with trauma-stricken eyes, then went back to staring into the corner.

Max opened his mouth to say something, was slapped by another Nun before it could come out. The sting was agonizing beyond reason. But he had been about to say, "How did the sex card go?" which would have earned him an even worse retaliation from his sister, even tied up.

Why *had* he sniffed those bicycle seats? He knew the answer but didn't want to admit it and he couldn't deny it: it was compulsion. Was it physiological, or purely mental, or a mental compulsion that had effectively mutated his brain chemistry so that it was physiological? Either way, to admit to it was to admit that he was a prisoner in his own body, his own mind. Something about the smell triggered his entire being with such barbarity that he would even sniff bicycle seats to get at it. He had read in a book once about baby cuckoo birds which "fool" the parent birds of other species which, flying back to their own nests with food for their own babies, then see the red, gaping mouths of the cuckoos and fly over to deliver their food to them instead. The red, gaping mouth itself is a stimulus so powerful that it can control the nervous system of other species of birds to their own detriment. Wasn't that red, gaping mouth really just like…

But other men didn't react like Max did, did they? He must have had an exceptional sense of smell. It had made everything about this mission especially taxing. Even now he was looking at the face of one of his abductors and admiring her Arabic beauty. In other circumstances… Why couldn't he stop himself? Worse, his eyes travelled down to her crotch, right in front of his face and started fantasizing about things entirely irrelevant to the situation.

The mental stimulation triggered a burst of nitric oxide in his brain, which, acting as a neurotransmitter, caused the muscle enzyme guanylate cyclase to produce the messenger chemical cGMP (guanine monophosphate), which in turn increased the size of the vessels carrying blood to the penis and shrank those which carried blood out. The influx of blood created pressure in his corpora cavernosa, causing tumescence, and shaming him to no end.

Oh, god! If only he could access his Casio! In his mind he even had a kind of stupid junior high school romance with Zilal. Where was she anyway?

No. He had thought too soon. He caught a glimpse of her walking past the open back door of the van, machinegun strapped over her shoulder and dressed in her khakis. She shot him a look as she passed that was so malevolent it forced all those puppy love thoughts out of his mind as if it were a pumped stomach. *"His nose was his enemy!"* he sang before being struck silent again.

One of the two Nuns in the van pointed at the feet of their three captives and said something in a language Max didn't understand. The second skater barely nodded, pulled a coiled length of twine from her pocket, and tied Smith's feet. Then she knelt in front of Tanuja to tie her feet, but Tanuja head-butted her with a sickening crack, then stood and delivered a reverse kick that launched the skater out the back doors – an incredible amount of force given the low roof of the van – but Max had seen it coming as soon as the rope had come out of the woman's pocket, because he knew Tanuja would be compelled to react. Now a herd of Nuns stampeded into the van with a trampling of Stormtrooper boots, shouting at each other and pinning Tanuja down. Finally, order was regained. Her legs were secured and she was shoved back up on the bench in a seated position while the surplus skaters exited the van again.

Why couldn't she help herself, Max wondered while also considering all the patching up she needed. For the same reason *he* couldn't help *himself*, he realized. It had all gone wrong somewhere. Something had rewired them.

She had walked the same circle over and over again, until she'd worn a trench in the ground so deep it was the only path she could ever walk anymore, around and around and around. And it was too deep for her to ever come out of again unless someone reached down and pulled her out. And one day, eventually, she would be too deep even for that.

And yet he still believed he was the one thing keeping her tethered to the shores of humanity. If she even *was* human anymore. And if there was any hope of a sexual miscreant acting as any sort of conduit to salvation for a homicidal lunatic. But then, if you head-butt your executioner without any hesitation does that indicate the absence of rational thought, or, in fact, in some way, its presence?

The van door slammed shut, the engine rumbled to life, and Max heard the voice of a man he didn't recognize in the front seat that sounded like he was talking about "Mr. Vain" by Culture Beat. When he looked across at Tanuja, he saw that she hadn't heard any of it because she was asleep.

***

They didn't get driven out to the strawberry fields or the apple orchards. They didn't get driven down to the river where the beavers lurked just under the surface of the black lapping water. To Max's relief and bafflement, when they were yanked back out of the van, for some reason, they were at Willie O'Ree Place, the arena where Pete Smith's roller derby matches were held. Combined with the invigorating fall night air, to Max it felt like a reprieve, maybe a stay of execution. They wouldn't murder them at the arena, would they?

The parking lot was empty. But another van had pulled up with them, and Gaddafi's Nuns, armed like Texas high school teachers, poured out the back of it. There was a third van too, but there was no activity around it. The three prisoners were hauled into the venue and slammed down onto the front row of bleachers. The lights came on with heavy metallic clanks. Tanuja took the opportunity to wake up and look back and forth in a confused daze. In other circumstances it would have been comical. Somebody would have made a gif of it and it would have been all the rage for upwards of three days.

Govinda Banerji dragged a folding chair across the floor, scraping the steel against the wood. His coat looked too warm, even for the fall. He set the chair down in front of the captives and sat down in it. Something about him was so hawk-like, that he was incongruous. Max was gripped by the fear of death again. Was he going to die here, sitting on bleachers in a place that looked like it could have been any high school gymnasium?

Banerji looked at them for a long moment, rubbed his jaw, adjusted his posture. Behind him, several of the Nuns were getting dressed in their bout gear. "This is bad," he said, "and this is good." He paused again. "Now… maybe this could have all been handled differently. I'll admit that, but it is what it is, and things got rougher than they needed to be maybe, and…" He had to stop to chuckle at Tanuja. "Okay, Miss Ramachandran, I know why you're looking at me with such incredulousness, but the point I am trying to get to here is that this was all supposed to happen much more smoothly, you know. Even after I found out Don Pendleton's Indira Gandhi was going to be here," waving his hand like a wing tip at her and looking up so they couldn't see the veins on his forehead, "you know, I thought she could still be dealt with with relative ease." He forced a smile. "Unfortunately, Dr. Balu fucked that up. That guy, you know, sometimes I could just –" He leapt out of the seat and made wild stabbing and slashing gestures in every direction, many of them in non-vital phantom body parts, before sitting down again. "Anyway," he smiled that smile again, "I need him, you know. Best in the biz, as they say. You know he once worked closely with that renowned rocket scientist APJ Abdul Kalam. And then Kalam became president! A scientist president. India is really the most remarkable country sometimes, don't you think? Anyway, Srikanth Balu didn't get to be president though. Haha! What's more, he tells me he spoke to you at Pete's party and it didn't even click who you were. Indian academics are often blind like that. What's your excuse for not recognizing him, I wonder?" He stabbed the air multiple times again. That too would have made for an excellent gif. "Oop! Speak of the devil."

Balu approached pushing a trolley of medical and lab paraphernalia. He had thrown a lab coat over the suit he'd been wearing for the cocktail party. "I can hear every word you say," he said through his teeth. "Can't you hear your voice reverberating all over this place? And I thought," he muttered as an afterthought, "you said she was 'a complete erotic.'"

"I know, I know," Banerji smiled. "I'm only teasing you, old friend. Besides, you thought she was dead, right? Wasn't that your excuse?"

Balu glanced at Tanuja then looked away, as he had done every time since they caught her, and fiddled with the gear he had wheeled in. She assumed he was embarrassed by his failure to recognize her. But he realized now that his hunch about her being a carrier of the MAOA gene was probably right, and that from the moment she came out of the womb she never really had a chance. He actually felt kind of sorry for her.

Tanuja for her part had by now already gotten over *her* failure to realize who he was at the party and only curled her worm-like lips at him. The ridged scar across her chest pulsated with searing, vengeful anger in his direction.

"You see," Banerji said to the prisoners, "I can insult him to his face all I like, and he'll just take it. Isn't that right, Balu? Because Balu is a man that needs to work, whatever it takes. The man's a genius, yet his own country has condemned him, and only people like me can give his hands the activity they need, expensive activity. So he has to put up with me. And we have you to thank for that too, Mr. Smith, or more specifically your money. I'm sorry I haven't introduced myself yet, but I suppose Little Miss Murder Bags over here has already done that for me, yes?" Smith made no word or gesture. "I thought so," Banerji continued. "Anyway, all of us have something we need to do, that we are compelled to do. Some of us, like Tanuja the Dismemberer over here need to get in my business at every opportunity, it would seem. Some of us need to sniff bicycle seats," he wasn't even looking at Max when he said it. "And one of us… needs to be the master of this country."

"You're going to assassinate the Prime Minister," Tanuja said.

"It speaks!" Banerji laughed, throwing his hands in the air. "Now about –"

"At the parade tomorrow?" she continued.

"For fuck's sake, I was in the middle of a sentence, *thevidyia*! You know, I really… I really just want to *kill* you, like this! Like this! Hyah!" His mime weapon of choice was always the dagger. It was becoming more Freudian with each demonstration. He sat back down and ran a palm over his scalp. "She thinks she is a *maharathi*, you know? The most masterful of warriors, so she can talk to anyone as she pleases."

"Why Canada? Why not India?" she interrupted again.

His eyes flared, but he answered. "Too hard," he said. "Why do you care what happens to this country anyway? I've pulled lint out of my foreskin with more integrity than the government of Canada! In any case, as I was saying, about the good part. The good thing is since you're still alive, it makes it easier for us to do a last test before the main event. So you're going to put roller skates on, you're going to have a match against my friends here, and at the end, if they haven't already killed you, I'll shoot you dead. I'm not really in favor of the idea of seeing a demonstration this way, I think it's ridiculous, but Balu the snowflake over here insists on such testing conditions. He's a scientist, so he needs his controls, and things like that, etcetera. And Mister Smith here, his obsession is so pathological that even in the face of death he's thinking, 'Oh, boy, I get to see some roller derby.' He can't help himself!"

"Actually…" Pete began.

"Shut up! So, anyway, you see? You want me to explain everything to you – how, why, when? No! You'll be dead anyway, so why do you need to know any of that shit! Let's just say, I have a small penis, so I have to do air daggers all the time and take over whole countries. People like you, Mr. Lakshmanan, you're lucky: you've never wanted to take over *anything*. Your dong must be huge." He did air daggers again, but as he sat down Balu was clearing his throat to get his attention.

"Oh, shit," Banerji said to Balu. "Let me guess. *You* want to explain it all, don't you? You all need to get over yourselves!" He looked away from Balu, tried to ignore him, and succeeded for two to three seconds before he shouted, "Okay! Fine" and wandered off exasperated and looking at the floor.

Balu wheeled his trolley in front of the chair and faced the captives. He still seemed to be avoiding direct eye contact with Tanuja, but he adopted a professorial air with hands behind his back, looking over his glasses. "The thing is," he began, and glancing around to make sure Banerji was out of earshot, he became emboldened, "all this roller rinking round and round business, all this politics, this is all nothing! What I've achieved," he nearly spat, "is the *most* important thing!" Max recognized the voice as the same one that was talking about "Mr. Vain" in the van, but it seemed so implausible.

Balu picked up a test tube with black specks in it, and held it aloft. Behind him, some of the Nuns were now ready and doing warm up laps around the track. He had to raise his voice to be heard over the coursing wheels. "This," he intoned, "is *Monomorium santschii*.

It's a very unusual species of ant. It no longer has any worker caste. Instead the *Monomorium santschii* queen enters the colony of another species and emits a pheromone which confuses the workers of *that* colony into thinking *she* is their actual queen. In other species, such as *Bothriomyrmex regicidus* and *Bothriomyrmex decapitans*, the invading queen would kill the host queen herself. In this case, the actual biological queen of the workers is now perceived to be an outsider, an intruder, and the workers proceed to then use their jaws to saw off the head of their own mother themselves."

Max and Smith stirred against their bindings. Balu paused to inspect the faces of his students and saw that Tanuja was not looking at him but staring with fixed gazes at Flora circling the track with the muscles of her back flexing like a jaguar's.

"Correct, Miss Ramachandran," Balu said, finally looking her in the eye. "After months of lab work and related field testing at the Smelly Smelly Cinema downtown, I have re-sequenced the pheromone for use on humans. Now," he shrugged his shoulders, "does it work the same on humans? No, of course not. But it will have a definite effect on those around an Alpha Female. And, maybe if I had more time…" He sent a resentful stare in Banerji's direction. "Well," he said, shaking off his distraction, "timelines get accelerated, science always comes second. And frankly, Miss Ramachandran, you hurt my baby boy, and I will be very happy to see you die here today."

Banerji returned, lifted the test tube of ants from Balu's hand, clasped him by the shoulders and turned him away in the direction of the trolley. "That was a fine performance, Balu," he said. "Thank you. You two really hate each other. Where is your little bundle of joy anyway?" Banerji asked. There was a tinge of bitterness in his voice.

"In the van," Balu returned with suspicion.

"Why don't you go get him?" Banerji asked. "I'm sure he would love to do some roller skating too. I know those boys you provided me with last year greatly enjoyed being physically active until Miss Murder Buckets here killed them all."

Balu hesitated before he muttered, "Okay," and walked away.

For an instant Max thought they were talking about some revenge thing. Balu had a teenage son who went down the wrong path and Tanuja had – for once – been merciful and at least spared his life? But something about the exchange made Max's spine and shoulders go cold – why was the kid in the van? – and he looked at his sister for strength, but she had seized up. Now he knew it wasn't a "boy." He looked the other way at Smith, who looked as confused as Max had at first. Unfortunately, even that was cut short.

"Balu is a very *sneaky* fellow too. He kept secrets from me. I thought his strange little baby boy was *dead*," Banerji said before changing tack. "Okay, Mr.

Smith," Banerji said, clasping his hands together. "You're up next. Now, now, there's nothing to be nervous about," he said as he pulled Pete up to his feet by the elbow. "All you have to do is explain the rules of the game, for my benefit and Torture Tanuja over here. And her brother too I suppose. You see how respectful I'm being, to you and to Balu? Yay, roller derby, right?"

Banerji gave Smith a shove, and he stumbled into the position vacated by Balu. He looked about as pleased as a film historian forced to discuss Citizen Kane at gunpoint in Guantanamo Bay. Meanwhile, a cadre of Nuns came up and surrounded Max and Tanuja. While the rest kept machine guns trained on them, two of them yanked off the prisoners' shoes and tossed them aside as though they were rummaging through a garbage dump, then replaced them with roller skates. Then they slammed helmets onto their heads like they were playing whack-a-mole to win.

"Okay," Smith said, clearing his throat. "It's easy, see – What... the... fuck...?" Balu had returned with the Monkey Man of New Delhi, bandaged all over and brushing the fur on his forehead with upper arm, loping along beside him on a leash. The thing shot Tanuja an evil look when it caught wind of her scent, but apparently Balu had good control over him because he didn't start flinging shit everywhere, and he stayed at the other end of the court with Balu and his trolley. Balu even seemed to be explaining the roller derby rules to the creature himself.

Smith's heart was pounding and he was having to take deep breaths. He'd had panic attacks before, when he was younger, but this was worse than any of that. He was even a bit feverish and pale. Tanuja looked bad too, but maybe all that training as a mercenary was being put to good use and keeping her centered. It was strangely Max who looked the least physically perturbed, though streams of sweat coated his sideburns. But Smith was also possessed by a rage at this whole situation, a boiling urge to violence he'd never felt before. It was all he could do to suppress it. He managed to muster the will to continue, even though Tanuja was paying attention to the thing instead of him. "Two teams of five at a time, skating around the track in the same direction. The game's made up of 'jams' that last up to two minutes, and you fit in as many as you can in two 30-minute periods." As he said it, he realized it was unlikely any of them would still be alive an hour from now.

Even before he could finish the thought, Banerji interrupted. "An hour? Fuck no! Haha! They play to ten points."

Smith gulped and continued. "One player on each team is the Jammer. They wear a star on their helmet that's on a thing like a bathing cap. It's actually called a panty. The other players are Blockers. Only the Jammers score points, and they get one point for each opposing team Blocker that they pass. So her own

Blockers will try to help her through, and the opposing Blockers will try to stop her. A Blocker is allowed to block her opponents with her hips, butt, or shoulders. Blocks to the back, tripping, and elbowing are illegal…" He looked over at Banerji in the chair. He was sitting still with an amused smile on his face.

Smith composed himself again. "You start at the starting line with two rows of four Blockers for each of the two teams. The two Jammers start side-by-side behind those two rows. Once the whistle blasts, everybody starts skating, counterclockwise. Now, during what we call the first pass, no one can score. The first Jammer to pass all the Blockers in the pack becomes the Lead Jammer. On subsequent passes, both Jammers start racking up points. The Lead Jammer can call off the jam before the two minutes are up whenever she wants. The only other thing you need to know is about the Pivots. One Blocker on each team is the Pivot. She wears a stripe on her helmet. During the jam, the Jammer who's not the Lead Jammer can pass their star to the Pivot Blocker so they swap roles. Most points wins. Actually, ten points wins," he corrected himself. He wiped the sweat from his jaw. "Any questions?"

In fact, Max and Tanuja had nothing but questions, but the three of them just stared at each other with a mix of disgust, horror, and – somewhere – anticipation. It was all so insane, maybe there was a chance in there somewhere that they would come out alive if they could just get it over with?

"We need more players for *our* team," Tanuja said, directing the statement at Banerji through pale lips.

Banerji stood up, and pushed Smith in the chest so he stumbled and fell on his ass. "I've taken that into account too," Banerji said. He snapped his fingers at one of the Nuns, who then exited the building. "You see how accommodating I'm being to all this nonsense?" he harped.

"Why don't you leave him out of it?" she said, nodding her head sideways at her brother without looking at him. Max was taken aback by the gesture – it might have been an expression of a glimmer of empathy, though only measurable in Planck lengths. "He's hardly an athlete," she continued, her voice low and gritty. "If you want a demonstration of how 'roided up you've got Gaddafi's virgins now, what point is there having him in it?"

Banerji wagged his finger at her. "Mr. Lakshmanan here is the whole point," he said. "Think how loyal he's been to you despite the train wreck your life must be, and all the reprehensible shit you've done." He gave Smith a playful kick in the shoulder, forcing the millionaire to scuttle away. "And yet, has he ever not been there for you? How many times have I shot you, only for this fool to stitch you up, wind you up, and set you walking again? What kind of doctor heals a murderer only to murder again? How loyal he must be. Think what a triumph it will be when he himself tries to strangle you out on that track."

Tanuja chose this very moment to barf all over the floor. Max and Smith both stared at her with concern and revulsion. She had managed to not get any bile on her sari though. But maybe, Max thought, her vomiting was a tell of sympathy too, proof of that human iota still in her.

"*Asingam!*" Banerji whooped in mock disgust, but he was laughing. "Maybe you should ask why I'm bothering with *you*," he said.

"Why should I bother doing this for you at all?" she asked.

"You're right," he nodded. "How about this? Mr. Lakshmanan will wait here with a gun to his head. If you break the rules on the track, he gets it. I'm going to kill *you* either way, but win and *he* lives. We'll still have a great show, as you shall see in a moment. Anyway, as I was saying, tomorrow we won't have to lay a finger on the Prime Minster. The citizens of Fredericton will do the deed for me, tearing him to pieces like confetti at his own parade."

"Ah!" he said as the Nun who had gone out came back in with some of the homeless people Tanuja and Smith had discovered under his house. They were in shackles, their faces despondent, and Bolo was among them. Their faces lit up when they saw Tanuja, their one-time savior, but the Nun yanked their chains back.

"See? They love you too, and they're all beefed up as well, much like the men I had in Montreal that you were so unkind to. So it's all fair, you see. You're the one person who showed them any iota of mercy for months now. So now they're as loyal to you as your doctor here is," Banerji said, "for now." He got up and went over to oversee the homeless people getting geared up.

Max hissed at his sister. "What the fuck's the matter with you?! Are you going to be able to do this thing? Have you ever been on those in your life?" he asked looking down at her roller skates. His train of thought had gone from her sanity to her physical prowess in an instant.

"It's been a long time, but, yes," she said without looking at him. "And I've seen Xanadu eight times." A drop of sweat lingered on her chin, then dripped off into infinity. Two Nuns skated up, and lifted her by the elbows, and they all rolled towards the track, the wheels of their skates echoing through the venue. Another Nun came over and hauled Smith off the floor and back onto the bleachers, then stayed there with a machinegun trained on him and Max. Tanuja was gone but the fading smell of her puke lingered, wafting up off the floor. It was suffocating.

The two Nuns who'd extracted Tanuja glided into their position as Blockers along with one other, who wore the stripe, and, beggaring belief, the Monkey Man as their fourth. Behind them was Tanuja's own team in a row of four. Burly Bolo was her Pivot Blocker. The others looked back at her with a mix of sympathy and resignation. Still, they were in their ready positions, and it seemed they knew what they were doing on the track, like Dr. Balu brought them out here regularly. And they were almost drooling in anticipation of throttling the women who'd been beating, whipping, kicking, and abusing them on a lark, some for months. Bolo looked confused, but perhaps able to follow everyone else's lead. Bolo was also the wobbliest of them on the skates, other than Tanuja.

Beside her was Flora, now in Heavy Flo mode. She looked like a hundred and fifty pounds of destruction, an unholy slab of meat in a Philadelphia freezer hanging there for Rocky Balboa to come practice against in an extended training montage if only it didn't hit back like a ten-ton hammer. She gave Tanuja a smirk when the mercenary looked at her, the first thing approaching a smile Tanuja had ever seen on her face. She was giving off a heavy, musky smell. Another drip of sweat plummeted from Tanuja's chin, and the start whistle blasted the same instant it hit the ground.

17

On one hand, the sole purpose of the film's roller derby conceit seems to be entirely so that it can revel in excessive violence. Yet, at the same time, it turns out that if you throw in motorcycles and cannons, the roller derby business is the least offensive thing about it.
Review by David Manning of *Rollerball* (1975) in Cahiers du Cinéma

It was a rough start. It took Tanuja a second or two to get rolling, but that was more than enough time for the orderly lines to transform into a mess of limbs. The homeless Blockers did their best to block Flora, and Bolo hip checked one Nun so hard she hit the floor almost before the start whistle stopped blowing, but the other three Nuns pincered into the line up to form a funnel for Flo to roll through. It was not a dynamic process, more like heavy flows of sludge forcing itself into new shapes, but, three seconds into it, two short whistle blasts signaled that Heavy Flo was already the

Lead Jammer. It may have been the shortest First Pass in Roller Derby history.

Through the throng of bodies Tanuja saw the Monkey Man's furry elbow and a corner of his 30-year old t-shirt up near the front of the pack, seemingly oblivious to the carnage behind him. And that *thing* aside, in the back of her mind, Tanuja could already see the damage these other half-animal women could do in the parade crowds tomorrow. Seconds into the game, they were panting, nostrils flaring, veins standing out on their necks, grinning every time they hip or shoulder checked one of these strung out homeless skaters in their hospital gowns. And she didn't even know what Flo herself was capable of yet, but there she was, already a quarter of the way around the track ahead of the Pack. Further around the corner, she caught sight of Max in the stands, seated bolt upright, face like a bare skull, and with a machine gun muzzle pointed at his temple. Pete for his part looked terrible.

She needed to put all of that out of her head and just skate, skate through this jumble of arms and legs trying to jostle each other out of the way. One of the homeless skaters – she couldn't have been older than fourteen – managed to get enough momentum to knock one of the Nuns stumbling back, creating a gap that Tanuja ploughed right into. "Come on! Get in, get in!" her teammates shouted to her. She managed to get past the second Nun by pure luck, but the one Bolo had knocked down earlier was waiting for her near the front of the pack, and shouldered into her with preternatural strength as Tanuja was on the verge of passing her. Tanuja stumbled, stumbled again, fell into a swamp of flesh, righted herself, got checked again, then fell. It only took a second for the pack to leave her behind. Down on one knee, she looked up and saw her homeless team still endeavoring to forge a path – or a gap at least – through the Nuns for her as the pack skated on. Tanuja lurched back up to her feet when a gust of wind shot past her. No. It was Flora. She plowed into the mob like a bowling ball, and by the time Tanuja got herself back into the fray, Flora had already exited it. Four points to the Nuns, plus a bonus point for lapping Tanuja, but right at the front, the teenager gained a burst of speed, screamed "Take it!" and hip checked Flora by surprise, sending her to the ground.

Flora rolled back into an upright skating position, remarkable considering her boulder-like physique. And then an odd thing happened. She skated over and touched the teenager high on the shoulder so her index finger pressed against the exposed flesh of her neck above the hospital gown. There was something about the touch, lingering. The teen looked at Flora and Flora mouthed some words at her, then skated off, beginning another lap. The teen looked back through the throng at Tanuja. Her expression was unreadable, but Tanuja caught sight of Banerji on the sidelines and he at least gave her a smile and a two-finger wave.

Being out here on the track, more and more of the rules started to come back to Tanuja from the night they'd watched the game and from Smith's incessant rambling during the time they spent together. On the edges of her awareness, it occurred to her that – amazingly – the Nuns seemed to be following the rules. Smith had drilled it into them – the one thing he could be counted on not to screw up, and she was grateful for that small victory. Her own team was a bigger problem. In a sense, their unpredictability and unruliness had caught the Nuns by surprise and prevented them from forming a dependable strategy at first.

But as Tanuja crammed into the Pack, one of the homeless – a middle-aged Mi'kmaq woman made especially hirsute by Balu's treatments – punched one of the Nuns full in the face. The ref whistle blew and the Mi'kmaq woman obediently skated off the track for her minute in the penalty box. Her head was doing a happy little dance independent of her body.

Even without the Mi'kmaq woman to help the other homeless Blockers, Tanuja managed to pass three of the Nuns. In the instant that she passed the third one, there were only the Monkey Man to the left and the homeless teenager to the right in front of her. She needed to pass the Monkey Man in the next instant before the Nun Blockers caught up with her. The Monkey Man, four feet tall, smelling like a sewer, and covered in small white bandages all over where the shattered glass had cut him, may have been Tanuja's other advantage. He appeared to be enjoying skating along at an easy pace, tufts of fur poking out of his skates like spring grass, and almost oblivious to the snarl of bodies happening right behind him.

Until he spotted Tanuja coming up behind. He snarled and veered right to check her but stopped himself short: even this little freak of nature somehow knew that checking in a clockwise direction would have been illegal. Instead he zigzagged to her seven o'clock corner, roller skate wheels screeching and was about to slam into her when the teenager barreled in from the right yelling "Fuck!" and collided with his hip, sending them both out of bounds and leaving an oily stain on her gown off his fur. It opened a clear path for Tanuja to catch up with Flo, but it was just dumb luck: the teen had been aiming for Tanuja, and she knew it. She needed to catch up with Flora before she made skin-to-skin contact with any more of the homeless team.

She got low and started to pour on the speed. Her red and violet sari coursed around the track like the Ganges filled with a thousand burning corpses. Out of the corner of her eye she saw Smith and her brother again. Max was watching wide-eyed. When he was behind a desk or whatever, she hardly noticed him. Now, with a gun to his head, she felt like there was an invisible tether connecting them, she felt things she hadn't felt in years, and the deal she had made to get him out of the orphanage and into a good home flickered through her thoughts. She began to understand – or at least felt like she should have tried harder to understand – all those laughable lectures he'd given her over the years about morality or trying to live a normal life. The dry finger on that trigger made Tanuja sicker in her stomach than anything on the track.

Further ahead, Balu was prowling the edge of the track with a grim expression, making notes on a clipboard and reading a stopwatch.

Tanuja skated towards the pack as fast as she could. She surprised herself and Heavy Flo too, who had heard her skates rolling up from behind, but veered left too late to check Tanuja, and only brushed her with a "Damnit!" Tanuja wobbled, like a three-wheeled auto-rickshaw about to tip over. But she caught her balance and shoved herself into the rear of the pack again, passing one Nun and earning one point before Flora tapped her hands on her hips to signal she was calling off the jam to the refs. The whistle blew and everybody stopped.

They lined up again as they had at the beginning. Even the Mi'kmaq woman came out of the penalty box and back onto the track. It hadn't been a minute yet, but there were small red streaks on her gown that looked like blood smeared off knuckles. Maybe she'd punched her guard and they couldn't be bothered to argue. "What's your name?" Tanuja asked her from her hunched over position behind the line of Blockers.

"Lucy," she said, her voice throaty but clear.

"Ha!" Flora laughed, the sound like the report of an elephant gun. "This will be the shortest friendship ever!"

Bolo was on the far left, in front of Tanuja and beside Lucy, the teenager was on the far right, and an old man with a dirty white beard was to her left. His mind seemed far away and his sad eyes blinked like a flickering light bulb. He was almost a write off, but Balu's treatments had given him unnatural strength and he had put up some fight during the last pass, even if he wasn't quite sure what he was doing. Tanuja imagined he had somehow made his way to Fredericton from somewhere further up north like Bathurst or Newcastle hoping for better homeless conditions down here in the province's capital. What a shame.

Tanuja leaned forward to whisper in Lucy's ear. "Don't let her touch you," she whispered. Lucy nodded, the whistle blew.

Flora catapulted into the two rows of Blockers, as it imploded into a clump, like somebody'd switched the gravity on, turning it into an instantaneous Anna Nagar traffic jam. This time Tanuja squeezed herself in quick too, but the rules had started to go out the window. People were starting to throw elbow checks. Flora attempted to grab Lucy, but Lucy ducked out of the way and Flora got the old man instead. "Protect me!" she yelled at him. The old man and the teenager took deep breaths through their noses, inhaling that odd musk that was wafting off of Flora, then lunged at Tanuja. Tanuja tried to dodge, stumbled on her wheels and fell. It was Bolo and Lucy against three Nuns and two of her own. The Monkey Man was still skating to his own beat, probably waiting for Tanuja to come to him. He was almost like a pace car, making sure the Pack stayed together – if the Pack got too far from each other, then the Blockers wouldn't be allowed to engage with each other or the jammers. But, could that animal-thing really be that strategic?

Lucy was obviously a scrapper, though, who must've seen her fair share of knock-down-drag-out fights in her time. She dispatched two of the Nuns with a knee to the gut and an eye gouge respectively. Bolo didn't have the enhanced strength of the others, but the injections he *had* gotten had already given him some prolonged endurance and he had his lumbering mass which he just kind of blundered into the old man and the teen like Fredericton roller derby's answer to Tor Johnson. It created enough of an opening for Tanuja to get up and hip check the third Nun out of her way. The Monkey Man heard wheels behind him, turned in curiosity to look, and she kidney punched him as she raced past, zipping right up to hip check Heavy Flo, who was caught by surprise and veered out of bounds with a curse and a grunt. Tanuja sped ahead, and looking back over her shoulder saw Flora pass the star to the Monkey Man. Tanuja was the Lead Jammer this time though.

The Monkey Man broke away with tremendous acceleration. His breathing made a noise like there was a corroded tin can lodged in his throat from a 1930s Our Gang one-reel. Tanuja could sense him gaining on her. Outside the track Banerji, Balu, Smith, and Max came into view again. Tanuja tried to ignore them, but she could feel the invisible tether between her and Max stretching thinner and thinner with each circuit.

The Monkey Man swerved into Tanuja's back with his shoulder – an illegal move that would have earned him thirty seconds in the penalty box under normal circumstances. She almost skidded out of bounds while the Monkey Man coursed ahead, a helmeted fur ball on wheels, like a 21st century version of Big Daddy Roth's Rat Fink, and gained so much speed that he was able to perform a legal apex jump over the corner. It was a perfect arc through the air, like the one on that rooftop in New Delhi, and the one in that derelict service garage just a day ago. He wasn't far from the Pack, which was now only distinguishable from an LA riot by the lack of people fleeing the scene with flat screen TVs.

Tanuja had to make the call: call off the jam now to avoid the Monkey Man scoring points, starting a new jam, and possibly ending up in the same situation; or, letting it continue and maybe scoring some points herself. And if she could get Flora away from the pack, she might be able to figure out if less exposure to her pong would mean a looser grip on the homeless skaters she'd affected. And would it work on her, or would it have no effect on another Alpha Female? But the invisible tether tugged on Tanuja's being, and she decided to go for the points. She hunched her torso and fought against the track, against the whole universe, straining to reach light speed.

The Monkey Man disappeared into the fray. Bolo and Lucy strained and struggled to hold him back, but they were blasted off course like billiard balls by the hips, shoulders, and illegal elbows of the other Blockers. By the time they righted themselves, the little freak was already past them. Seven points. The teenager and the old man were trying to hold him off too, until Flora cried out, "Let him through, let him through!" They hesitated, conflicted for a moment, then let the other Nun Blockers shove them aside for the Monkey Man to pass. Nine points. "Pass it! Give it!" Flora said to him, and he whipped off the star and passed it to her with a cartoon frown. She took off with such elemental power that by the time Tanuja reached the pack, Flora was already half way around the track, a murderous hurtling juggernaut.

The Nuns had managed to form a rear line across the width of the track, blocking Tanuja's entry. A tried and true strategy, but Tanuja slipped and wiped out, and with the hospital gowns behind them trying to break up the Nuns' defense line, one of the Nuns tripped over Tanuja's helmet and hit the track like a wrecking ball, shattering her jaw. One of the other Nuns went to her. Tanuja used the opening to roll over and get back to a standing position to enter the gap in what was left of the pack. Flora was on the exact opposite end of the track, and thankfully for Tanuja the teenager and the old man were muddled, less bloodthirsty as they tried to block Tanuja's way, not sure why they were doing it, for the moment anyway. So proximity to Flora's smell did matter. The old man even backed off, and turned his attention to getting the Monkey Man out of Tanuja's way. The three homeless managed to fend off the Monkey Man and the remaining Nun so Tanuja got through. She repressed a shudder as she left the Monkey Man behind her. Four more points, bringing her team to five. But she tripped again, her body slapping down on the track. The teenager was looking at her with renewed interest. Even Tanuja caught a faint whiff of Flora coming. Almost prostrate on the ground, she looked back over her shoulder and saw Flora darting towards the pack, faster, faster, like a shark. Tanuja needed to get back up and tap her palms on her hips to stop the jam before Flora could enter the pack again and score that last lethal point. But she was so fast, so fast. Not human. A lightning god.

Tanuja struggled to get back on her feet, but it was over. She knew it was over. She gritted her teeth with strength like a steel vice to keep her entire being from spilling out. The teenager was starting to move towards her. Still looking back over her shoulder, Tanuja saw Flora make skin-to-skin contact with Lucy and Bolo. Now the pack started to flow towards her as a whole. It didn't matter. Flora skated past Lucy, Bolo, the old man.

The red digital numerals of the scoreboard flicked over to twelve points.

Banerji gave a hand signal to the skaters. They all glided up to Tanuja and held her in place. Her teeth were still clamped shut, sweat poured off of her face. She struggled, but it was futile. Banerji smiled, walked over to Smith, pointed the gun at him, and shot him in the chest. The body slumped over on the bleachers with a reverberating thud, like a four-year-old who fell asleep at a late night game. Banerji smiled from ear to ear. His satisfaction was palpable all the way across the room. The Monkey Man applauded like a trained circus animal, entertained by the sound of the gunshot.

He pointed the gun at Max and pulled the trigger. The Casio VL-1 was a toy keyboard so small it could fit into Max's suit jacket pocket. The bullet shattered it, then shredded a hole through his heart. His body fell backwards into an awkward configuration, like a forgotten rag doll. The thread that connected him to Tanuja snapped apart in that instant.

Tanuja screamed to the skies – an unholy, chthonic sound, the sound of a Nietzschean abyss. The skaters dispersed and let her drop to her knees, and it all went out of her: her brother, the strand that linked them, the giant Dali with the clouds hanging in the gallery downtown, the slow motion Montreal streets at dusk, Pete Smith's cabin in the autumn light dappled by red and orange leaves. Not even the voice of the Rani. Everything gone, all gone, until nothing was left except that obsidian black neutron star at her core, spinning at five hundred revolutions per second. But the weight of her grief was crushing it, pushing it past the Chandrasekhar limit until it collapsed on itself and became an anti-space, a sucking hole of nothingness that was her entire being at that moment and forevermore.

She did not even hear Banerji's steps on the track, was already a non-person by the time he lifted his gun and shot her in the chest and she too fell on her face, dead.

18

For certain is death for the born
And certain is birth for the dead;
Therefore over the inevitable
Thou shouldst not grieve.
The Bhagavad Gita, Chapter 2

Tanuja was on the set of "The Golden Girls" (1985-1992), but rather than being in Florida, it was a strange pocket of civilization in the middle of the wilderness. She knew this even without being able to look outside. And, the more she thought about it, the more she realized the house was not even a house, but a campaign tent. The ladies were all sitting around on the living room sofas. Max was there too. Estelle Getty was Max's sweetheart so he was sitting very close to her on the couch. When Tanuja saw them all there in the living room, and they all looked up at her, it was uncomfortable.

Her sari was white with brown and green stripes. There was something rustic in its simplicity, a village sari. She looked down at her hands and she could feel the weight of them. The real weight of them. And there was a real soreness in her chest where the bullet had gone in, but it was nothing compared to what it would have felt like if she hadn't taken the injection. So this was no afterlife, she wasn't even fully unconscious. It was a lucid fever dream. She had flashes of memories: Zilal's face as she woke, those muscle-hard arms hoisting her up, Oilers Toque Man pulling Pete Smith onto his feet, her brother's corpse behind them as they walked away.

The unlikely, sonorous beeping of an ECG monitor from the real world resounded through the room. How could she not have known that he was involved with Estelle Getty? In fact, did she know anything about him at all?

Well, she knew that he was dead.

"How were you sure he wouldn't shoot you in the head?" Rue McClanahan asked.

So they knew about that here. "I wasn't," Tanuja answered. "But he's cautious. And in my case he's afraid of me. I gambled on him not getting too close, and from a distance the biggest target on a person is their torso."

"You don't belong here," said Bea Arthur. She was tall, dignified, elegant, the most powerful of them all. She had an air of Benazir Bhutto about her. The words stung, particularly coming from her. When her brother repeated them, she realized they were true. No old age and domesticity for her. No even being human. She shot up Balu's formula and she was something else. But it wasn't really her brother. It was her mind's shade of him, trying to push her away from this. He was dead. Why did she have to leave? Couldn't she stay here? Why *couldn't* she have this life? He was dead. Hadn't she done enough? She wanted to dissolve into the very dust and become nothing, end her time here, but their gazes fixed her in place.

Tanuja was overwhelmed by the urge to escape from their admonishments before anyone asked how she knew Pete Smith wouldn't get shot in the head. Because she didn't. There was a large fish tank to the stage right side of the set next to the tent's main exit that was never there on the actual TV show. Some fish were in it, bobbing against the glass like idiots, as if either trying to find a way out, or trying to comprehend the invisible solid. She projected her consciousness into one of the fish, a tiny trout, and swam out the rear of the tank, which had no back but kept going and going, into the ocean. It was easy to become the fish because she was already an animal, the least thinking animal, even before the injection.

And so she sped at incalculable dream speed through that strange, dark blue and gold world with swarms of her brethren around her, until she saw the white line of a beach edging a tropical rain forest above the sunlight-speckled water line. She accelerated towards it and became a massive tortoise, still scampering onto the land with the speed of a Nintendo character rather than of a Testudine. And when she hit the trees she was a wild boar, hairy and lumbering, but fast, more a product of the Sega generation, smashing through the underbrush with her tusks, trying to get as far away from The Golden Girls as possible. Then she was walking upright, a kind of half-creature like the Monkey Man, but muscular and leonine, covered in fur, her tusks shrunk into her fanged jaws, capable of exerting three hundred kilograms of pressure. But this phase was short-lived. As she left the forest behind and entered a desert, she became a human child: her own self as a child. Growing as she ran, she became an adult, and then there was no sign of the forest anymore. The dessert was vast and uninterrupted, the sands an almost uniform mélange of gold, yellow, and brown, with gargantuan dunes cresting and falling like ocean waves. A silent wind coursed across the sands and through the folds of her sari.

"I made up a new song. Do you want to hear it?" It was Max's voice coming down from up on the sand dune behind her, as high as a two-story house.

"Don't," she answered, looking up at him. He was silhouetted against the sun behind him.

"Okay, I'm going to sing it."

"Don't," she repeated, a note of warning in her voice.

His Casio began to bleep and bloop. It was a bigger one – sixty-one keys.

"*Dey*! I fucking warned you," she said with a big sister glare.

"*I got shot right in the nipple! Would've preferred some raspberry ripple!*"

She tried to scramble up the dune to wrestle him down, but it was a vain effort. The sand would have no part of it and slid her back down in shame. Max laughed so hard, first at his own joke, then at his sister's pratfall, that the crest of the dune gave way under his feet and he went down too. For him, this was the worst that could have happened because it put him within arm's reach of her. She picked him up and flung him into the air like a frisbee and he disappeared into the horizon, his scream trailing into silence. So gravity was different here. Sometimes. She hadn't meant to throw him that far, but it didn't matter: an instant later he was there beside her again.

"Are you just going to stand here?" he asked. "Aren't you going to avenge me?"

She looked through her kaleidoscope but everything in it was wrong, drippy and gloopy instead of angular. "What do you care? Would you even know about it if I did?"

"No. Well, do it to satisfy your own rage then. Why stop now? I thought that's all you were made of. Like a lump of play dough."

She hesitated before answering. "Maybe it wasn't."

"Maybe it can be."

Strangely, a school of trout of the kind she was

before was swimming under the sand. She didn't answer him.

"You can't just sink into the sand here and blow away into nothing. And you can't stop running. You want to turn back and run around on all fours again? Hide in a hole? That's an animal kind of a trick. You need to keep going, and run all the way back to the city. If you don't, no one is going stop Banerji. You think he'll stop with Canada? The people who can destroy a thing, they control it."

"What will I care? I'll be dead, like you."

"What about saving the world!"

"Is it worth saving?"

That stopped him for a second. "Probably not," he answered. "Well," he continued after a moment, "Balu and the Monkey Man are still alive."

She looked at him. "Balu and the Monkey Man are still alive," she repeated at him.

"Heavy Flo is still alive."

"Heavy Flo is still alive." Something stirred deep, deep in the dead blackness of her being.

"Banerji killed me. Banerji killed *you*."

That did it. It welled up in Tanuja, compelling her to turn from her brother and bolt across the dunes at such speed that everything blurred around her. The city appeared, far off on the horizon. And by the time she reached the city's edge, she was a warrior god with a machine gun in her hands, another slung over her shoulder, a pistol in her purse, and a knife strapped tight to her ankle so it didn't chafe as she ran. Her streaming sari was almond, coral, crimson, honeydew, pearl, caramel, lavender, titanium white, and persimmon. It was a fire streaming behind her as she entered the city, until it burned away and all she was left wearing was a hat made of cheese she'd made herself.

She ran to the hospital, bounded up the stairs to her floor, flew into her room and threw herself on the bed, into the hole, the Tanuja-shaped void that she'd left behind in the universe, slotting perfectly into it like it was the last piece in a quintillion-piece jigsaw puzzle – just in time for her to wake up in the real world.

***

She opened her eyes to see Zilal looking down at her, and her arm shot up with the speed of a Scud missile to clutch her throat. Zilal gasped and her eyes bulged. The beeping of Tanuja's ECG monitor accelerated. Eyes red and popping, Zilal managed to pry Tanuja's fingers off one by one, until the air rushed back into her throat with a wind tunnel roar. "Jesus fuck!" she said between coughs. She slapped Tanuja's arm out of the way. "I saved your ass, you know, and this is the fuckin' thanks I get?!"

A nurse came into the room to follow up on the change in the ECG, but Zilal turned and told him to fuck off and he scuttled away like a shit-eating sewer rat.

"Anyway," she continued to Tanuja, "I suppose you really saved yourself. Can't believe you injected that shit into yourself… *and* Smith. Jesus! What the fuck were you thinking?! That shit could've killed you. Another dose, and some fucked up shit – *irreparable* fucked up shit – would've probably happened to your system for sure. How does it feel to have hair on your tits now anyway? Happy about that?"

Tanuja spoke. "Why were you looking at my tits in the first place?"

"Number One: I saved your life, and that's all you've got to say to me? Number Two: You wish. Someday, Prince Charmin Flushable Wipes will come along and – Ganesha willing – maybe he'll finger blast you in his Kia down by the river. Until then, please, think about your tits on your own time."

"You're the one that brought it up," Tanuja said looking down the front of her hospital gown. Fortunately, there was not actually any hair on her tits. Just that massive and gnarled purple and brown rocky mountain range scar. "You could've helped me before I got shot. Where am I?" she asked.

"Yeah, I didn't shoot up with monkey steroids and it would've been very conspicuous if I showed up there uninvited. You're in Dr. Everett Chalmers Regional Hospital. Pete Smith's money and connections scored you the best care anywhere. He used to patch up his old team's bruises and broken bones here and have them track-worthy in no time. That was before Balu came along. We repatched you with military-grade sutures and state-of-the-art liquid bandaging. Your brother he, uh," she cleared her throat, "he did a pretty decent job on the previous stuff though. I guess that shit in your system will flush itself out since you only had one dose."

"How long have I been here?"

"Holy Shit. This must the most riveting conversation I've ever had in my life. About twelve hours. It's eight a.m. The parade starts at noon. There's a lot of activity going on at the house. If they're going to assassinate the Prime Minister, you need to tell me what you found out. Is it going to happen before the parade or after?"

"During."

"Come again?"

"Didn't you get briefed?"

"When I heard the rumblings that you'd been taken to the arena, I slipped out the first second I could. I haven't been back since."

"So you decided to finally break cover the one day we actually needed you on the inside the most?!" Tanuja berated.

"And your sorry ass is alive. Glory, glory, hallelujah. Talk."

"Balu has weaponized ant pheromones to affect human emotions relating to loyalty. Flora is the carrier. Whoever she touches and stays in chemical range of will turn on her enemies. I think it was even making the Nuns skate in tighter sync with each other. She'll get the citizens of Fredericton to either protect her while she and the other Nuns kill him, or get them to do it themselves."

"Fuck… me…" Zilal said. "Jesus, the team's got a float in that parade, for fuck's sake. I'll call the cops and warn them," she said, pulling her phone out of her fatigue pants.

"No," Tanuja interrupted. "If you warn the cops to stay away from an assassination attempt on the Prime Minister, they'll do the opposite and try to apprehend her and probably end up pulling the trigger themselves."

Zilal shoved the phone back into her pocket and clenched her jaw. "Well, we've got another few hours before the parade starts. Some time for you to get some more rest. Well, enough for *you* anyway. What's your next question, Speak & Spell?"

"Where's Pete Smith?" they both said at the same time.

"He's in the room next door. He'll be fine too. Got hair on his tits though. Now listen to me." Zilal sat on the edge of the bed and spoke in a slow, low voice.

"The thing that happened to your brother was fucked," she said. "Totally fucked. I didn't really know him, but he seemed like a decent guy for a milquetoast. And I know right now you probably want to just lie here until you disappear, but actually Balu and Banerji and all those others are still out there, and you need to get up and –"

"It's killing time," Tanuja said, yanking out the IV

and clambering out of the bed.

Zilal got up too. "Shit. That was easy. I rehearsed this whole fucking soliloquy you wouldn't even believe. Don't you at least want to hear my closing line?"

Tanuja paused and looked at her.

"It was, 'And that's how a bill becomes a law.'"

Tanuja took a step towards the door.

"Wait!" Zilal said. "I got your bags out of storage. It's all here." She pointed at the suitcases in the corner. "You're welcome. I would say, 'What'd'ya got in there, bricks?' except I know how much heavy ordnance weighs."

Tanuja swung one of the bags up onto the bed and opened it. It was packed with neat stacks of folded saris of every color and pattern conceivable. Zilal hadn't seen such an explosive array since the last time she went to Pothys sari emporium in Chennai. Tanuja picked out a red and cream number with three wide bands of repeating chrysanthemum patterns across the top, waist, and hem, and got dressed as if she was in the room alone.

Then, with more effort, Tanuja swung the next bag onto the bed. The top level was a foam insert tray with slots carved out to perfectly fit each piece of the staggering arsenal that was in it. It was filled with heavy artillery, black and glimmering like beetle shells. Though she'd seen it that night in the motel, the sight of it still inspired a sniff of admiration from Zilal.

Tanuja pulled this tray out, to reveal one underneath full of a range of dazzling bladed weapons with exotic curves and ornate handles the likes of which Zilal had never even imagined before. If they'd been made of plastic they could have made even Latoya Jackson blush.

From this selection, she picked out three items.

A Keralan *urumi*: also known as the "whip sword," a sword handle and guard with four steel whips emerging from where the blade would be. A weapon that had taken her years to master.

A *chakram*: a steel rim-shaped disc throwing weapon with a razor-sharp outer edge. This particular *chakram* was fifteen-centimeters in diameter – not especially large, but still Tanuja's weapon of choice for decapitations, much as it was for Vishnu.

A 17th-century *chilanum* dagger, its forty-centimeter blade gently curving away then coming back again, its handle a stylized flower carved from ivory. This was an unusually large example, almost a sword. Tanuja had a scabbard for it that she tied around her waist.

She put the firearm insert back in place and picked out a semiautomatic Vittsjo 9mm. It was small enough to fit in her purse along with the *urumi* and *chakram*. She slung the bag over her shoulder and looked at Zilal to get out of her way.

"I guess I'd better go gear up too," Zilal said, her voice pummeled into inadequacy. "The parade starts at the exhibition grounds," she said before leaving. "It'll make a circuit through downtown, covering the length of Queen Street, and passing city hall there, where they've got a special platform set up for the PM and local officials to watch the show. Then they're having a fancy-schmancy lunch on the Pioneer Princess IV. It's a local riverboat for proms and shit."

"The attack will happen during the parade, not on the boat."

"I agree.

"Queen Street..." Tanuja mused. "Then they'll pass the Smell-O-Vision?"

"Yeah."

"Meet me on the roof there at noon. I'll need to stop at K-Mart before I go over."

Zilal nodded her acknowledgement and left.

Tanuja went next door to look in on Pete Smith. The nurse who had tried to interrupt Zilal earlier was in the room with him, but he left as soon as Tanuja looked at him and he saw the scabbard she was wearing.

Smith was weak as a rag, but he was awake. She could see the lump of the bandages on his chest pushing up his hospital gown. He was on oxygen and an IV drip too.

"I had the strangest dream," he croaked when he saw her.

"Me too," she said.

"I'm so sorry about your brother. Zilal told me."

She nodded.

"I suppose I should be amazed you're up and walking around, but I'm not in the least. I don't actually feel that bad myself. Just like I got punched in the chest real bad. Still nauseous too. I guess that injection's worn off for us though, but those women, the test subjects… They're past the point of no return, aren't they." It wasn't a question. He said it as a plain statement of fact, his voice full of regret.

"Yes," Tanuja replied.

"Could've won a hell of a lot of games with that stuff," he said aloud before realizing he shouldn't have. "I really fucked up," he admitted with a sigh. "But you saved me anyway."

"Yes," she said. "You did. But there are worse crimes than wanting to cheat at roller derby."

"Are you going to kill them all?" he asked, looking at the sinister *chilanum* fixed to her waist.

It took Tanuja longer to answer than he expected. She sat on the edge of his bed, and when she began to speak, it was as if to herself. She supposed Max would have wanted her to just tell Smith everything. So she tried.

"Why are they doing it? What's in it for them? What do they gain? Nothing. Nothing except Balu's approval and above him Banerji. And before them it was Gaddafi. Zilal was a double agent, undercover for years, so steadfastly loyal to the RCMP. Why? What was the point? And she was in so deep and for so long,

I began to wonder if she started to feel loyal to Banerji too. And had she felt that way for Gaddafi too, and maybe to you as well? Why did she skate so hard? Why did any of them? Was it to impress Banerji? Or was it to impress you? Why were they all loyal to men? Why be loyal to an army or a country? Why be loyal to anything? The whole time I've been in this town, I've been wondering what their fathers were like, what their mothers were like too. Why have I been avenging the deaths of my family for fifteen years on people that had nothing to do with it? Why am I letting Nadhini Shastri choose my assignments? Why can't you shut up about roller derby? Why was Max the way he was?" She paused. "Even without Balu's serum, we're all just ants, all in the same witch's brew together, swirling around and around. To answer your question," she said, while images of her husband and children and Max flashed through her mind, "I'll do what my ant brain tells me I need to do."

19

||||| ||||| |||

Entry from Tanuja Ramachandran's mission journal, October 17, 2013

The inside of the Qarnage Queens float was a purgatorial sweatbox: cramped, dark, and hot as fuck.

It was parked at the Fredericton Exhibition Grounds, hitched to a truck that would haul it through the streets. The grounds were an empty lot for most of the year, except for two weeks every September when it became engorged with fairground rides, carnies, cotton candy, and projectile vomit flying everywhere at unpredictable trajectories. Now it was a hub of frantic, bustling activity as Fredericton's various organizations put the finishing touches on their floats and got in their costumes. Mothers Against Fredericton Masturbators (MAFM) had assembled a particularly impressive float considering that the death-by-jerk-off crisis had only been in the media cycle for less than forty-eight hours. The mothers had wrangled their sons, some as old as forty, to stand around on the float wearing nothing but oven mitts, their briefs, and duct tape over their mouths. All the school marching bands were there, the equestrian clubs with their horses, a contingent of tractors no one had any interest in seeing, least of all the nation's Prime Minister, and the society for creative anachronism dressed as knights and squires, among dozens of others.

But the Qarnage Queens prepared their float with a silence and sobriety that seemed to radiate a cloudy menacing energy that deflected the high school cheerleaders and curling teams that crossed them from interrupting them with pointless cheerful banter. Their display was painted cardboard cutouts of the wildlife of Tripoli. None of the locals would get it. Some of the skaters would stand under the "palm trees" and wave.

The float was almost twice as elevated as anyone else's, because inside it was a Trojan horse housing ten of the skaters and the Monkey Man who were already in it. Flora had been shocked to learn that Balu had been hiding this thing in the woods for more than a year, that he had even been feeding homeless people to him at times. She had known that the Monkey Man of New Delhi was Balu's handiwork, but, like everyone else, had thought him dead. (*How old was he?*) But now she was sitting right next to him. In the minimal light that beamed through the cracks and air holes, she could see him staring off at nothing in particular, his furry chest rising and falling. The smell in the box was diabolical. Ten sweating women, the surviving homeless people, plus the Monkey Man's fur, and, Flora had to admit to herself, the pheromones she herself was giving off. Anyone else would have been compelled to burst panting out of the box, but these women were trained to endure worse tortures than this. Indeed, some of them had. Flora herself had suffered four days in the hands of Iran's Ministry of Intelligence and sometimes in the night she woke up thinking she was still there in that black limbo, a four-by-four cell with no windows and shit and piss all over the floor. And, except for that last detail, it was much like this place.

The Monkey Man reached into his jeans pocket and pulled out a crumpled paper bag. She heard it rustling in the dark. He pulled something out of it that glinted for an instant in the minimal light then went in his mouth. He took a deep breath, then ate another one. The pause before the next one was like clockwork. This time he stopped mid-motion as it was travelling to his mouth as he caught her eye staring at him.

"Poppins?" he offered in that ridiculous voice of his. Some of the others looked up when they heard it in the near dark.

She shook her head, and he shrugged and popped it into his mouth like a little burst of sweet light disappearing into a black hole. She heard the bag scrunch up again and get shoved back into the pocket.

"You… like sweets?" she asked. She wasn't sure why she was trying to make conversation with it, but there in the dank, sweaty box it started to dawn on her that it was sort of a brother or an ancestor. Balu, in a way, was father to them both.

"Mm. Last Starfighter likes Poppins." He sounded thoughtful about it, but like he had nothing more to say about it or any other subject. Perhaps this was the extent of his intelligence. But then he added: "Also Lucky Charms." So there was more. There was some uncomfortable rustling from some of the others in the box when the Monkey Man spoke.

"Do you have a name?"

"Only Last Starfighter. Good name. Outer space name."

"Do you… Do you know what you are?"

He thought about it a second, brow furrowed. "What strong lady mean?"

"My name is Flora," she said. "I mean before were you a… a boy, a person like us in here, or were you like an animal like you see in the woods or in a zoo?" Did he even know what a zoo was? The fact that she didn't even really know how to talk to it became more glaring with every word out of her mouth. She was even starting to speak as slowly as him.

"Always outer space," he answered with the wisdom of a Zen master.

Either he didn't understand her question, or – not impossible – he didn't know the truth himself, but she pressed on anyway in that halting manner her voice had adopted. "No, I mean," she said, "Doctor Balu made you… right?"

He answered with one word: "Daddy." Then: "Is daddy your daddy too?"

"I was just wondering that," she muttered. There was some rustling around the box again, but the smell Flora was radiating seemed to be keeping everyone muted and subdued, like they were hardly there. "No," she said to him, "My father died a long time ago, far, far from here. I remember him being strong and caring, but irrational. Looking back, I don't think I've ever really understood him."

There was silence for a moment, then the Monkey Man said, "Now, tall bird face man is your daddy."

"No," she said. How did he know about Banerji? "But…" She hesitated a long time, almost leaving the thought unfinished, before continuing. "I do believe this life is the only life, and to be here, to experience the near impossibility of being alive for these brief moments is the rarest most precious fluke, like winning the lottery. And that *win*, that precious jewel is the one thing, the only thing we have. And so the worst thing any person can do to another person is to interfere with their moment here, because it's all any of us have. But many people have done that. Whole countries have done it. And only people like Banerji and… some before him, even my father in his small way, have tried to see justice done for that."

The Monkey Man hadn't understood any of that and was only matching up the shapes of Lucky Charms to their colors in his mind. But as the truck that would tow them through the parade rumbled to life and began to pull the float behind it, he said, "You smell like Last Starfighter too."

***

Tanuja was crouched on the roof of the Smell-O-Vision, and scanning the parade through her binoculars as it crept up the street. When she heard the horse's hooves behind her, at first she didn't turn. "Where have you been?" she asked.

"This is good," said Lakshmibai. "It hasn't been like this for a long time. Just you and me. It needs to be this way. The British were treacherous, but they were nothing like these villains. Your brother…" Tanuja finally looked at her, but the Rani's expression didn't falter. "… was like a cartoon devil on your shoulder, luring you away from the path. There is only one way. Nothing less will suffice."

Tanuja turned back to her binoculars and saw the Queens' oversized float turning into the street in the distance at parade-crawl speed. She pulled out her phone and dialed Zilal. "Where are you?" Tanuja exclaimed. "They're coming around the corner!"

"I'm right behind you," Zilal answered on the other end.

Tanuja turned to look behind her just as Zilal burst

261

out through the roof access door into the cool air. The second she did, the Rani disappeared.

Tanuja stashed her phone and demanded, "What the hell are you wearing?!"

Zilal was in full RCMP dress uniform except for the boots – she was wearing her roller skates instead. She was also armed with an AK-47 which was not standard RCMP issue. She ignored Tanuja's question and instead pointed at a cream 2003 Bajaj Chetak motor scooter parked in the corner, India's answer to the Vespa. "Where the fuck did that come from?!" she cried.

"I stole it from the hospital parking lot. Must belong to one of the doctors. I had one in Madras twenty years ago."

"And you rolled it up the stairs?!"

"Just eat the mangoes, don't count the trees," Tanuja answered.

Tanuja passed her the binoculars, and Zilal spotted the float. "Jesus," she mumbled. "I've seen facial herpes less obvious. Can't be comfy though. Banerji won't be in there."

"I agree. He'll be watching from somewhere safe, and not getting his hands dirty. Always at a safe distance." Tanuja popped two wake-up pills in her mouth before continuing. "You can bet Balu's somewhere discreet collecting his precious data too."

Zilal scanned the crowds lining each side of the street with the binoculars, but couldn't spot either of the two men. Then she scoped the float again, and said, "What the hell are they wearing on their feet? Those aren't regulation roller skates." She passed the binoculars back to Tanuja, and Tanuja looked through them.

"I don't know," Tanuja said. "You'd know better than I would."

"I've got a plan," Zilal started to say.

"I've got a better one," Tanuja interrupted. She had a backpack beside her that she wrenched open, and pulled out a $14.99 super soaker that she held out to Zilal. Zilal recoiled and gagged, dry heaving at the acrid stench of it. "What the fuck?!" she cried.

"I filled it with Smell-O-Vision sauce. Anyone Heavy Flo touches, spray them. Maybe it'll overpower the pheromones coming off of her. Get *her* if you can. I'll try too. They'll be attempting a brute force assault. Chretien's security will be too tight for a sniper attack, and there's no vantage point in the vicinity anyway. But Flora will want to recruit as many locals as possible to form a wedge for her, so they won't leave it till the last minute. We strike as soon as they show themselves. Too early and we'll lose Balu and Banerji, wherever they are. Minimal civilian casualties that way too. We can always elect another Prime Minister. But the more *other* people die, the less point there is."

"I agree."

"And whatever happens down there, Balu, Banerji, and the Monkey Man are mine. You're going to have to kill some of your fellow Nuns. Can you do that?"

Zilal nodded. Tanuja guessed it would help that she was back in the RCMP uniform.

"Shoot them in the head," she continued, "or they'll just stand back up again."

"I know that."

"Good. Now get on the back of the Chetak, side saddle."

"But what…" Zilal was interrupted again, this time by a resounding thump and a collective gasp from below.

Three sides of the float had slammed open, hinging downwards and hitting the street, and the skaters were pouring out of it, streaming in curlicue arcs towards the Prime Minister's dais. As soon as Flora emerged, she shoved her hands into her shirt and rubbed them on her armpits, shoved them down her pants and rubbed them on her snatch, then started skating through the crowds and smearing her juices on the faces of everyone she could reach. For a moment, the confused crowd thought it was just an odd part of the parade, but then the sight of the Monkey Man triggered screams, panic, and people stumbling over each other to get away. He was delighted and started clawing at anyone in his path for fun. One person he caught by both arms, then ripped them off like the ends of a wish bone.

Then the Nuns opened fire on the Prime Minister's security detail with their toe-triggered roller skate guns, and the crowd's desperation to disperse became truly frantic. The skaters went beyond anything seen on the roller derby track, going into full figure skating mode. They performed Biellmann spins, butterfly jumps, cantilevers, Charlotte spirals, and midair leg wraps, creating perfect fractal *rangoli* patterns of bullets. It was like the most disappointing Disney On Ice ever, topped off with everyone's ice cream scoops falling out of the cones at the same time.

"It's on!" Tanuja said. She slung her purse cross shoulder, ran to the scooter, and hopped on, not waiting for Zilal. She started to back it up with her feet. It was then Zilal saw the plank Tanuja had set up on the lip of the roof. She hopped on the scooter too.

Tanuja revved the Bajaj, hit the gas and flew off the ramp crying, *"Deeeyyyy!"* as they flew in a perfect parabolic arc, like a stone flung over a lake. They pounded onto the street right between the Queens' float and a Boy Scout troop right behind them.

Zilal rolled off and started splooging people in the face with the super soaker. It seemed to work, as they stopped chasing after Flora, fell out of the group, and stood there looking confused. Some of them even started making out with each other. There were two Nuns coming at her, performing simultaneous twizzles, but Zilal had trained with them so long, she knew exactly the trajectory they would take and how they would duck and dodge. With the AK in her other hand she strafed to her left and perforated the two

Nuns like postage stamps, and almost got a third, except this one spun around and started shooting bullets out of her skates. Zilal barely evaded them, not even having enough time to curse. She shot another one in midair like she was skeet shooting humans. Just like Tanuja had said: chest shots didn't matter – if she didn't shoot them in the head, they just kept coming.

Tanuja, meanwhile, had stayed on the bike, held the *chilanum* out straight from her side and simply rode past a Nun, slicing her body in half like it was butter, the torso sliding off the legs into a clump on the street. Jaiyana, the librarian, who delighted in the slaughter of Fredericton's homeless, with the arm Tanuja had broken last night in a cast: slashed across the throat. Ended. Kamilah, the Libyan native, who'd strangled a whole family to death when she was fourteen. Ended. Naomi, indoctrinated into a Japanese doomsday cult at age eight. Ended. Tanuja took a bullet in the leg and bit her lip through the pain.

Some crowd control cops pulled their guns, pointing them every which way in their shaking hands, but Flora got to one of them before they could get off a shot, and soon they were all shooting at each other after she touched another one, then more of them, inappropriately.

Tanuja was right, Zilal thought. They were going to have to do this on their own. Unless… Who were the four people in hospital gowns that had come out of the float? Their eyes were glazed and distant. They almost seemed to be in a trance. But how could she get at them? They were in the throng around Flora that was surging in the Prime Minister's direction.

***

As soon as the bullets started flying, some from his own men, Sheriff Greg Flynn had taken cover behind the crocheting club's quickly-abandoned float, and was making reluctant and separate shots at the other gunmen in sporadic bursts in between long sessions of cowering in despair. A motor scooter screeched up beside him. It was the tourist he'd had arrested and who'd showed up at Pete's party, and she was armed like the lovechild of a Navy SEAL and Conan the Barbarian.

"You?!" he said, sweat coursing over the veins on his forehead.

"Shut up, and go help the PM! Zilal and I will deal with this!"

"Zilal? You mean that RCMP officer with the super soaker?!" Flynn peeked over the float and saw what had happened. As soon as the first shots were fired, the PM's secret security gorillas had scrambled to get him off the stage and into a getaway car, but the Nuns on their skates had arrested their retreat to a crawl, swirling around and around them like they were tracing wrought iron lacework. Now, though, the security squad were within a few meters of the car, with the PM shrinking and covering his head in the middle of the black suit huddle as if his arms could stop bullets.

"How?" Flynn shouted over all the noise, but Tanuja had already sped off.

***

Another spray of bullets came at Zilal, grazing a shoulder. She spun and arced backwards on her skates, firing back and taking down another Nun – Xiao Jin Le, a woman she'd known for three years. She saw Tanuja further up the street, still on the scooter, cut off a Nun's arm and cut another one in half vertically from the crown of her head. Zilal creamed the back of the crowd around Flora with Smell-O-Vision sauce, and when the people she hit fell back dismayed and making out with each other, she plunged into the herd punching out civilians left and right until she had a clearer shot, then she lathered the crowd again, and this time managed to hit a few of the people in hospital gowns. If any roller derby refs had been present, they would have had a field day. As the gowned figures regained their senses, they bravely turned on Flora, but then the Monkey Man jumped on Zilal's head, slashing her back with his steel claws before she could spray any more. As he pushed her to the ground, the AK went flying out of her grip.

***

"How can she be alive?!" Banerji spat, while making wild, irate stabbing motions in the air.

"I suppose… she injected herself with something when they were snooping around in the lab," Balu replied. "How I would love to get a blood sample," he pined.

When the screaming and shooting started, they had run away like everyone else, but stayed close to the action and ducked into a nearby alley. Banerji had disguised himself in a flat cap and a long coat with the collar turned up. Balu was wearing a blonde wig and aviator sunglasses, but had not shaved his moustache because his Tamilian identity could not even conceive of the act.

"And how can just two of them be taking down our soldiers like paper dolls?!" Banerji cried again. "They're almost all gone! What the hell have I been paying you for?!"

"My work wasn't complete!" Balu defended himself. "And besides, the one in the RCMP uniform is one of ours!"

"What?!"

"She knows exactly how all the other women fight and skate like they were in the womb together! Perhaps the blame lies with you, Banerji," he said rapping a finger against Banerji's chest, "for screening them with your wing wang instead of your brain!"

"This is all your fault! I thought that monkey thing was dead! Killing Ramachandran is a job for humans not an animal!"

"Leave him out of this!"

Banerji winced.

"Damn it! He's going to get away!" Banerji wailed. He mimed stabbing the Prime Minister's handsome face, sweat trickling down his temple. Then, as if stuck by a bolt, he drew his gun and took a heavy step towards the ongoing battle at the PM's getaway car. "I'll have to do it myself," he ventured, but his eyes were full of dread.

Balu grabbed his arm. "No, Banerji, wait," he said. "There's still a chance."

***

Tanuja whirled the scooter around a hundred and eighty degrees and pushed it full throttle at the Monkey Man with her sword out. The creature heard the engine coming at him and leaped off Zilal, tumbling out of the way as the blade sliced off a tuft of his fur. Tanuja had to swing the scooter around with a ninety degree skid to bring it to a full stop, and when she looked back, the Monkey Man was gone. The next instant he delivered a flying kick to her shoulders out of midair, spilling her and the scooter clattering onto the street. He was on top of her the same moment, rearing a steel clawed hand back to stab her brain when Zilal sprayed him full in the face with the Smell-O-Vision slime. As he recoiled in frenzied disgust, Zilal picked up Tanuja's sword and slashed at him, taking three fingers off his left hand that clinked when they hit the pavement. He gripped the stumps and howled, then fled yelping with a three-legged gait.

***

Flora's mob were swarming the prime minister's security detail who were now firing wildly at civilians, veins bulging in their temples and necks, spittle dribbling from their stiff, terrorized lips. But they were winning through the sheer inescapable logic of guns vs flesh, until, through the throng – some of them trying to hold Flora back after being sprayed by Zilal – Flora managed to touch two of them, and shouted: "Kill the Prime Minister!" The pungent smell of her filled their nostrils, and they turned – to the horror of their comrades – on their own PM. The other agents had no choice but to open fire on them, just like the cops were still shooting at each other, and some started shuffling back into more strategic positions, while others started brawling with their fists. Flora made skin-to-skin contact with two more.

The PM was huddled and wincing through his teeth at the fracas around him when a thick arm shot through the tangled forest of legs and grabbed his wrist and dragged him out of the fray. It was Sheriff Flynn, armed with a pistol and garbage can lid that would be lucky to stop a marble fired from a slingshot. "Come on! Come on!" Flynn shouted, still half dragging the PM. A bullet hit the garbage can lid at just the right angle to ricochet away, but another hit Flynn in the thigh. They kept going, around to the other side of the car where the doors were more accessible. As Flynn opened the back door, one of the Nuns spotted him, but he shot her in the head and she fell back. He shoved the PM into the car, slammed the door shut, and shot another oncoming Nun.

***

There was a screech of roller skate wheels, and then a jet of noxious ooze sprayed through the knot of Secret Service men and Flora's horde. Zilal managed to hit the four corrupted security agents who now stood there half dazed. The civilians who'd been hit were either entangled fighting their own, or fled shrieking. "Get Chretien the fuck out of here!" Zilal yelled at the gorillas. This time they were lucky, and an instant later the driver's side door slammed shut, and the car with the PM in it sped off.

Half of Flora's minions went running off after it like mindless animals, the other remained to guard her and were about to attack Zilal.

"Wait!" Flora bellowed. Her posse stopped, panting. "I knew you weren't one of us," she rumbled. "You've ruined everything!" There was genuine sadness buried deep in that voice somewhere.

Flora looked at Zilal's weapons: a super soaker and a sword that looked like something Paris Hilton would use to harvest wheat. Zilal's eyes flashed down to Flora's skates with the gun barrels on them. Flora caught the glance and smirked when their eyes met again. She slid a bowie knife from her belt. "May thy knife chip and shatter," she intoned. It was a ritual taunt of the Revolutionary Nuns before blade-to-blade combat. Zilal knew it all too well, and had used it herself before many a kill. Zilal set her jaw, and assumed combat posture when Tanuja's *chakram* came screaming through the sky and decapitated Flora, her head rotating through the air like a head popped off a doll, like the head of Ganesha, betrayed by the man who was supposed to be his own father. Flora's screeching lackeys charged at Zilal, but she skated backwards, spraying them with the ooze nonstop and hoping the remaining security agents would hold off the surviving Nuns on their own. Surely Flora's scent would wear off soon too, she prayed.

"Ramachandran!" she hollered over her shoulder. "The riverboat!"

Tanuja looked over to where the boat was docked behind city hall. Banerji was charging up the gangplank and firing at the civilians there who'd been waiting for the party, while a badly disguised Balu followed close behind him holding the Monkey Man's spurting hand and patting its head like he was consoling a child. The passengers had thought they might be safe staying put on the ship, but now they threw themselves overboard in their tuxedos, jewelry, and all. Banerji had his gun against the head of the ship's pilot and it started to pull away from the jetty.

"*I'll* deal with *this* mess!" Zilal yelled.

Tanuja righted the scooter and gunned it a kilometer up the road to the Westmoreland Street Bridge over the river. The airflow whipped her sari violently. She turned up onto the bridge, and drove out until she was in line with the riverboat. Then she pulled the 9mm out of her purse and fired at the tires of the oncoming cars, turned and fired at the cars coming the other way, then shot out the bridge's railing in front of her with a heavy barrage.

She backed up the Bajaj, put the gun back in her purse, and waited, waited, waited. Angry drivers were starting to get out of their cars shouting. The ship came into ideal range. She revved the engine again and blasted off into the air, slamming down onto the Princess's top deck and rattling the tables with the lavish place settings that had been laid out on them for a lunch under the sun.

The Monkey Man pounced out of the shadows of the stairwell and clotheslined her off the Chetak, but she rolled with the blow and landed in a crouch, pulling out the *urumi* whip sword. She slashed at him and missed, but the noise it produced stunned him. It didn't require much strength from her as the four flail-like blades were energized by the centripetal force of the swing.

For a moment, when she saw his hideous, misshapen fangs, she hesitated.

I must not fear, she told herself. *I will permit my fear to pass over me and through me.*

She slashed again, and this time her aim was true. The Monkey Man didn't know how to dodge the sweep of it. He leapt in an arc, and this time she anticipated it, because he always leapt – it was his nature – and the whip sword caught him full in the chest, sending him to the ground with a squawk of searing agony.

The light dimmed as the ship passed under the bridge. The Monkey Man was shuddering, holding his chest with the hand missing three fingers, and holding up his other hand as if to plead with Tanuja to have mercy. But the scar across her chest tingled, and this time she didn't hesitate to approach him. She stamped a foot down on his burning chest to hold him in place, and tied his hands with a length of rope. Then she tied his legs together with another one. She tied a hoop in the other end, tossed it over a post, then hauled on it to make it tight. The Monkey Man was flailing, trying to lift her *chappal*-adorned foot off her chest, but she ground it in further. She tied a third rope around his neck, never betraying any emotion. He caught a flash of something shiny attached to the other end of this one. Grappling hook. "No," he begged, his voice almost human in the moment. But that was all he had in him. He knew there was no point.

The ship came back into full sunlight. Tanuja tossed the grappling hook with as much force as she could muster onto the railing of the bridge. It caught.

She backed up a few steps to watch with her pistol out, strands of hair escaping from her tight braid, and her *pottu* – her third eye *chakra* – now an ugly streak across her forehead. As the ship got further from the bridge the Monkey Man's body started to stretch out. "No, no..." he murmured. Gradually, the arrangement stretched and stretched him so he was seemingly floating at an angle in the air. He started to scream and scream, his sinews and flesh and fur and muscle pulling apart, until finally he was pulled in half at the bullet hole in his chest – his point of least integrity – with a revolting sound. The legs slumped to the deck, and the upper torso swung and dangled from the bridge, getting further and further away as the ship left it behind, and still wearing the lacerated Last Starfighter shirt. Tanuja's brother would have been deeply disappointed in her, but the Lakshmibai gave a satisfied sigh. She shot the rope and the macabre slab of meat fell into the river.

Balu screamed from the stairwell. Tanuja pivoted around and fired at him but missed. He disappeared down the stairs. Tanuja chased after him down to the lower level. This floor had been set for dining too. He was running down the aisles between tables, heading for the edge to jump ship like all the civilians had. "Stop!" she shouted. He froze in his tracks, and turned gingerly to face her.

She heard a click behind her right ear and spun to elbow Banerji in the head. She took the gun from his hand, threw it overboard, and shot him in the knees.

Then she strode over to Balu. He sunk to his knees in a supplicating pose, pulled off the blonde wig, and put up his hands. She pointed her pistol at his forehead.

"You know," he said, "it would be so stupid of you to shoot me. Did you know I developed a treatment that can cure meth addiction in one day? That's how I cleaned up those street dwellers. I needed them clean so I could work on them." Banerji was moaning in the background. "One day! And you want to take that away from the world? You want to take my genius away from the world? The world needs my genius in it, you ignorant –"

She shot him in the head, and his body slumped to the deck with no ceremony. His last thoughts as the bullet entered his brain were of Glenn Medeiros singing "Nothing's Gonna Change My Love For You."

She crossed back to Banerji.

"You killed my brother," she said to him.

Banerji thought for a moment, a puzzled look on his face. "That guy was your brother?" he said

It would be a long time before Fredericton's police organized themselves and caught up with the boat. She put her gun back into her purse and pulled out the other thing she had bought at K-Mart that morning: a twinkling $2.99 cheese grater.

And all up and down the St. John River, there was a mania of beavers slapping their tails against the water like judges pounding their gavels…

20

*A billion years from now, will the morality —
good or bad — of any human action have
mattered? Once the last human ceases to exist,
then it will be as if even the most deplorable
outrages ever committed on the face of the Earth
never happened in the first place.*
Akshay "Max" Lakshmanan, quoted in
testimony at his disciplinary hearing for the
embassy "Seat Sniffing" incident

Pete Smith stood in the garden of the Laura Secord
house, the maple leaves around him the most perfect
conflagration of reds, oranges, and yellows, and the air
was chill and bracing. He was using a cane for support,
but the strength in his back was returning, and he
could already feel that in another day or so he wouldn't
need it anymore. He held up an index finger like he
was holding an invisible teacup, and a Purple Finch
alighted from a branch to land on it. Smith whistled at
it. It twisted its head back and forth, looked at him

with animal curiosity, fluffed its wings, adjusted its footing, and then took off again.

Footsteps crunched up the gravel path behind him, and he turned at the sound. It was Tanuja, of course. Her sari was Vantablack, copper turquoise, and night frost blue.

He was the first to speak. "That was a hell of a show downtown yesterday."

She nodded. "I thought I might find you here."

"I wasn't so sure if it would be you coming up that path or the cops," he answered.

"I had a long talk with Greg Flynn and we agreed you had no knowledge – which is true. You won't be charged with financing terrorists. You recruited a roller derby team without realizing their true objectives – also true."

Smith adjusted his footing. "That almost sounds too easy. What does Greg get out of it?"

"He gets to be the hero of the story. He saved the PM from an attempted assassination, and saved the whole city and country, really. Plus, he has a dedicated RCMP officer to corroborate the whole story, probably the most dedicated RCMP officer there's ever been, in fact." Even Tanuja herself wasn't sure that she meant that as a compliment. "I'd dismantle that lab though. Discreetly. Replace your home security detail too."

"Jesus," Smith muttered at the ground, adding a sniff of admiration. Looking up at her again, he asked,

"Is this what it's like in your world?" He paused, then added, "Everything is bullshit, isn't it?"

She nodded. "That's true. Everything *is* bullshit." She thought for a moment, then said, "But that statement is not bullshit."

He thought about it too. "But if the *statement* is not bullshit, then that means *everything* is *not* bullshit. Which means that the statement *is* bullshit, which means everything *is* bullshit, which means the statement is not…"

"And on and on forever."

"What will you do now?" he asked

She looked around at the river sparkling through the trees, and the wind rustling the leaves overhead. It was the full flush of autumn, orange and scarlet. "I think I'm going to bury Max here. I think maybe he wouldn't have minded that."

"I can have that arranged," Smith said.

"And after that, I thought I might stay a while. It might be good to *not* be in that world for a while," she said looking at him. "At least until my next…" She stopped midsentence to check the phone that buzzed in her purse. She flipped it open and read the text message on its screen with pursed lips.

"What is it?" Smith asked.

"Mayor of Toronto needs to be liquidated," she said. "I have to go." The phone went back into the bag.

"Will I ever see you again?"

"I'll be back, she said. "That's a promise." Her face

was as unreadable as ever, but behind the glaze of her eyes lurked devastating grief over the loss of her brother. There were no guns in her purse, only her kaleidoscope and a photo of her family. She turned and went back down the path and the cool wind traveled through her sari like a desert breeze through the dunes.

***

Within a week, the first snow flurries came to Fredericton, and by late December every yard, every roof, and every tree in the city was covered in pillows of snow like something out of a picture book. Greg Flynn did indeed become a national hero and decided to take a very early retirement to go into private security. Zilal was posted to the RCMP branch in Vancouver and was awarded medals and commendations she'd never even heard of, but she kept them all in a shoe box tucked away in a top corner of her bedroom closet. She never worked undercover again.

And by the time spring rolled around, Pete Smith had assembled a new roller derby team of women from around the province ranging in ages from seventeen to forty-five, and of every shape, size, and color imaginable. They were fun-loving, determined, and unpredictable. Sometimes they didn't get along with each other, but mostly they did, and a few months later they were already one of the top teams in Atlantic Canada. He got medical treatment and jobs for Oilers

Toque Man and Bolo too, mostly gardening around his house or working at the arena's concession stand. He did the same for the Mi'kmaq woman and the teen girl, whose names he learned were Lucy and Viola, and the other people Balu had abducted. The ones who'd survived anyway.

And fall came again, and another winter and another spring. As the Earth went around the sun, so too did the skaters go around and around the track. And still he waited and waited for her to come back. But she never did, and he never saw her again.

ACKNOWLEDGMENTS

This book is the manifestation of my mid-life crisis in prose form, and it was written almost completely in secret over a period of five years. However, I am indebted to several people without whom its existence would have been even more unlikely.

I thank Katherine Atkinson, Koom Kankesan, and Emmet O'Cuana for enduring or attempting to endure this manuscript at various stages and providing invaluable feedback.

I also have to thank Tracey Hill for her undying and irrational support of my writing for more than twenty years.

Thank you to Chuck Greer for clarifying the rules of roller derby to me, and also my apologies for perverting them.

Thank you to my family.

Also, since this may be my first and last chance to mention them, I must express my gratitude to Demetres Tryphonopoulos for teaching me what constitutes good writing; and to Don McKay and Jan Zwicky for teaching me how bad my writing was, and, like a persistent boil, continues to be.

If you've made it this far, then thank you for reading it anyway, my loyal Fedaykin.